A GLOBAL PHENOMENON

7 HEARTBREAKS TO FIND ONE LOVE

Mistakes to avoid in Finding Love that works for all

DIPIKA SHUKLA BAIDYA

BlueRose ONE.com
Stories Matter
NewDelhi • London

BLUEROSE PUBLISHERS
India | U.K.

BlueRose ONE.com
Stories Matter
NewDelhi • London

For permissions requests or inquiries regarding this publication, please contact:

BLUEROSE PUBLISHERS
www.BlueRoseONE.com
info@bluerosepublishers.com
+91 8882 898 898
+4407342408967

ISBN: 978-93-5819-543-9

Cover design: Muskan Sachdeva
Typesetting: Rohit

First Edition: January 2024

Contents

Perfect Match

Still searching for a perfect match, true love, made for each other kind of partner but with a heavy heart and lots of disappointment and heartbreaks, I have to tell you that there are no such kind of things really exists in this world. What if I tell you that True Love is a myth and live happily ever after is a bullshit. You may ask then what about all those perfect couple. Then I must say that when we see a perfect couple; we can't guess their real efforts to keep the relationship, they have to work harder again and again to make their relationship perfect. Behind every made for each other couple there are so many sacrifices, adjustments with different opinions, behavior and personality. Despite of all, respecting each other is must.

Once there is a small town girl, named Sunaina, at her sweet sixteen phase, an age when she is neither a kid and nor a complete grown up. As 90's kids grown up early than their age, Sunaina also acts same at her 16, she behaves like an adult, from that tender age she has started dreaming of her prince charming. She looks pretty having candid hazel eyes, mid length dark brown hair, slim with plumpy cheeks and arms, having innocent face, sharp features, wheatish complexion, five feet five inch tall and carrying an attractive aura. She is crazy at heart but decent in front of all. She wants to live in her own way and follow her heart always to take any decision in her life. She believes in her dreamland and also believes that whatever she is dreaming of will be happened one day. She is straight forward while talking to others but quite sensitive also if someone speaks rudely to her. Those who are 90's kid, definitely can relate with her. Sunaina likes to read love stories and also strongly believe that someday she would have her own love story to tell others and her Mr. Perfect will come to take her to his wonderland. She is fan of 90's love story movies where a fascinating guy suddenly arrive to change the boring life of the actress and take her to his perfect wonderland.

Sunaina is pursuing her10th std. and like other teenagers she is also facing issues like board exam fear and anxiety, unmanageable menstrual cycles, newly introduced to lingerie, waxing, threading, hormonal break outs, which face wash and perfume to use and confusing career decisions and among all these chaos she is confused with one more feeling which we called "Love". She is being surrounded with friends who have boyfriends and so she also want to experience it for once.

One day, a guy from her class popular as cool guy, continuously staring at her. While he is staring her, she also noticed him and for the very first time she felt a very weird feeling, her hormones fluctuates, she felt blushed all of sudden and feels nervous without any reason. First of all she thought that may be this is love but later on she get to know that it is just an Infatuation and not Love. That guy who is staring at her continuously for a week, finally proposes one of her close friend. All these makes her more confused. She gets more confused and thinks that if he likes her friend then why he was staring at her and why she felt such weird feelings if he is not her Mr. Perfect. Except her all her friends have boyfriends and only she is single yet so she is more confused as she had never experience being in love how it feels. Although these happened to her, thinking of her career on priority, she moved on with no regrets.

Sunaina wants to be a doctor because her parent's told her to be a doctor from her childhood. She is noble at heart and have sympathy for poor people. She equally loves both kids and older people.

She is god gifted beautiful with innocent face and at her teenage when she realizes that most of the guys started noticing her and gets attracted to her then she has started taking more care of herself and become more conscious about her looks and clothes. And with time, she learn how to flourish that attractive aura with mesmerizing way of talking. From her teenage, she receives a lot of love notes from boys whom she doesn't considered as her perfect match. She had set a very high standards for her partner so she had ignored all these love notes and eagerly waiting for her Mr. Perfect to come.

She is pursuing her Intermediate final year with a dream of becoming a renowned doctor, parallely she is also dreaming of her Mr. Perfect. One day while sitting inside her classroom, she heard a guy (student) is telling to one of her friend about his past life, his worst family experience, his step mother and his loneliness, he is also telling that in his family nobody cares about him.

On the contrary, Sunaina is always being a pampered child and belongs to a joint family. She have her father, mother and a younger sister in her family. Despite she is elder among all siblings and her cousins, she is loved by all her maternal and paternal relatives and cousins. She can't even imagine that how one can be so lonely in spite of having family. She have never seen anyone's step mother in her real life. She felt sympathy for that lonely guy and with passing time, she has started taking interest in knowing more about his life, his pain and his each and every activities. She finds him very unique from rest of the boys in her class as she never had any friend having step mother. She has started asking about him from almost everyone in her class. She get to know that lonely guy, named Vinay, have limited friends and he never speaks much with anyone. He have his own swag and is handsome among classmates, brave and fights for truth, behaves equally with girls and guys, all these creates soft corner in Sunaina's heart for him. She have mix feelings of both liking and sympathy for him.

As she is an ambivert, she doesn't want to talk to him immediately. She is stalking him to know more about his lonely life and decided to help him somehow. She wants to support him so that he would not feel alone again. So one day in January, while he was in his practical lab, she came to talk to him for the very first time. She also bring gift for him and a friendship card just to make him realize that he is not alone in this world and she cares for him. Somehow he was aware of Sunaina from her friends who had already given him some sort of hint about her. He had already noticed her few months back about her caring nature, attractive aura and was also stalking her. After that day of practical lab, he has also started caring and protecting her from other boys and searching new reasons to talk to her. Few months passed like this, one day he proposes her in front of everyone and request her to say "yes" otherwise he will commit suicide. Sunaina said yes but she is not sure about her feelings for him. She is confused between love and sympathy.

Vinay have switched his group to her practical group and taken combine coaching classes. He has started liking her because of her child-like innocence, simplicity, damn care attitude and off course her pretty face. He praises her always and also cares for her. Day by day he became extremely protective and possessive for her which she likes. She feels pampered and safe with him.

Sunaina has been started enjoying her first experience of being in love and possessive nature that Vinay shows towards her. She has considered Vinay might be her Mr. Perfect whom she is waiting for. She flaunts in front of her friends because she have a boyfriend now and whom she thinks more handsome than her friend's boyfriend. Sunaina is fascinated with love stories shown in movies and books where the lead girl should be popular no matter how. So she also have the desire of being in limelight and popularity so that people around her talk about her no matter good or bad. Sunaina's friend circle are also impressed with Vinay, his personality and his intelligence. Like any other teenager girl, her dream comes true of being popular among friends after having a handsome boyfriend and on top of that who treats her like a princess and take her for date and gifting her on her birthdays, valentine's etc. Now she is having all what she had manifested for so long. She is happy to flaunt her life and love-story in her friend circle and make them jealous.

Everything is moving very smooth in her life and she is on seventh heaven until the day when Intermediate exam result comes out. She fails in two subjects which breaks her from within. She was a meritorious student and never fails in her entire life. Earlier she always got rank within top three. So after failing in two subjects, she even think of committing suicide as she can't face her family, neighbors, cousins and friends. It seems like her dream of becoming a doctor is shattered. And the more disheartening news for her is that Vinay had passed all the subjects. For a while, Sunaina become self-centered and stopped talking to him as she considered him the reason behind her failure. But after few days she realizes that what she was doing is totally wrong and her failure in academic is completely her fault and her carelessness attitude towards study. Now she thought of letting him go to big metro city for his further career because she realizes that love means sacrifice. And one should let the other partner go for his betterment and if he will come back then he is totally yours. Sunaina have extreme faith on Vinay even more than herself. So she forced him to go to the bigger city for doing MBBS and get the degree of a doctor and make her feel proud. Vinay also promised her that he will do the same and will wait for her to join the same MBBS College next year.

After one month, Vinay moved to Delhi for doing his MBBS which is a five years course and Sunaina stayed back in her hometown. As all her friends got admission in colleges, she became lonely and frustrated. Although by her parent's guidance, support and her strong will power, she again took admission to complete her twelfth but this time with more focus, she determined. After taking re-admission, she gets new friends in school but never goes for any outing with them and most of the time she spends in her studies only. Once in a week she talks to Vinay and both of them update each other's life plans and whatever happened in last 7 days. On every weekend, she keeps on updating him about her coaching, exams and her new friends. She told him each and everything what she did in the whole week. She told him everything even if she watches any movies, hang out with friends, whatever she did. While after few months, Vinay has started hiding things from her and telling her that he has no friends in college and he is lonely again like earlier. Sunaina is worrying for him and asked him to make friends. She always told him that as we are social being so we shouldn't live alone. Vinay never talk about any of his friends. This continues for the whole year. Finally Sunaina's exams over and results declared. This time Sunaina has passed with flying colors. She has been proven her family and herself that she is still a meritorious student. Her family feels proud of her and celebrate for her. She told all this to Vinay and asked him to wait for her as she will clear the entrance exams and will take admission in his college.

Immediate after her academic exams over, she has started preparing for the entrance exam. During this period, she forget to notice that Vinay was avoiding her calls. Whenever she called him, he shows excuses of being busy and hang up the call. Sunaina's new friends always told her that long distance relationship never last but

Sunaina never accept this. She had her own point of view that if love is true, distance doesn't matter.

In the mid of her entrance exam preparation, one day suddenly Sunaina and her friend decided to do prank call to Vinay to test his loyalty. One of her friend, Megha advised her to keep check on her boyfriend and asked her to let her do this prank call. Sunaina allowed her. Megha called Vinay and started flirting with him. Vinay gets irritated and talk rudely to her and tell her not to call him again. Sunaina feels happy after hearing this and told Megha that her boyfriend is loyal and her relationship is not like other distance relationships.

After one week of this incident, Sunaina got a call from a random number, she picked up the call and heard a voice from the other side, a girl is saying hello to her and introducing herself as Vinay's girlfriend, name Megha. Sunaina gets shocked for a while and can't believe to her ears. Within a minute, her eyes filled with tears and her vocal felt like chocked. Sunaina is shivering and nervous but to confirm she asked her again with her shaky voice, who's this? Other side's voice, "Megha this side and I am Vinay's girlfriend. I got your number in his mobile and to know who you are I called you". Sunaina still have faith on Vinay and thought that the other side girl is lying or might be doing some prank. She dropped her call and called Vinay to confirm and tell him about this random prank call. But Vinay didn't pick up the phone. Sunaina has been calling him continuously and her heartbeat gets faster and non-stop tears rolling down her cheeks. As she has blind belief on him, she called him non-stop with faith in her heart that Vinay will pick up her call and clear all these misunderstandings happened and also tell her that he doesn't know this girl "Megha".

She believed that they are perfect match then how is this possible that someone loyal like Vinay who have no other friends except Sunaina and is so much fond of her can also cheat her. She can't handle her emotions and is not possible for her to tackle the situation. For the first time she feels the pain of heart breaking. She can't even think properly. She is repeatedly trying to call him and messaging him but getting no reply from his side. Suddenly she realized that something wrong happened to their relationship and Vinay is cheating her. She locked herself in her bedroom and cried breathlessly for whole day and night. Her mind gets blank, not able to think anything and she became speechless after this incident. She thought that her life is finished now.

Suddenly her phone rang and OMG its Vinay. She has wrapped up herself and wiped her tears and took deep breadth with a ray of hope that he will say to her "*It's all misunderstanding and he doesn't know any Megha*". She picked up the call and says hello with a very low upset tone that generally happens after several hours of loud cry. On the other side of phone, it's completely silent. Sunaina heard a girl's voice in the background telling "*Vinay say the truth to her*". After hearing this Sunaina is in complete shock again and settled down on the floor. She has been started crying and also self-consulting that not to believe this voice. Few minutes later Sunaina stops crying and asked with a firm voice, is it you Vinay? Are you there?

Vinay replied yes, it's me and from today onwards don't try to contact me or call me anymore. Sunaina asked, what happen? Why are you saying like that? Vinay replied, I have a girlfriend, her name is Megha. Sunaina asked him, do you love her? Vinay keeps silent again and didn't speak for few minutes. From behind Megha asked, Vinay why are you so silent? Then Vinay with heavy heart replied yes I love Megha and you don't call me again. Sunaina hang up the call and put the phone down and her tears rolling down her cheeks non-stop and she recalls all her past memories with him. She felt herself like a stupid that how could she believe so blindly that she can't see a cheater in him. She thinks how fool she is. And still she can't believe that someone's feeling changes so easily. She has started realizing that love is a bullshit and she regrets her stupidity of falling in love with him and wasting her time and spoiling her career. She had wasted one year of her career for him. She did all possible things to maintain their relationship but in return she gets a broken heart and deception for her lifetime.

Moral: There's nothing like perfect match in this world. You have to make it perfect and for making it perfect, both have to keep working towards it every single day. No one of the two can take it for granted or else have to loose it forever. Love is a beautiful feeling but may changes with time and circumstances. If today someone have love feelings for you and loyal to you, it's not necessary it will stay forever. It may changes with circumstances and no one will tell you that we have to work for it to work it well.

Why do Lovers Cheat

Everyone have their own reasons to cheat their partners and there are always three versions of truth. First truth is of who cheats, second version is of who is being cheated and the third version is the real truth. Vinay cheated Sunaina because being a teenager Vinay wants to enjoy his life without any commitment and wants to make physical relationship with harmless innocent girls which he wasn't successful with Sunaina. On the other hand Sunaina don't want to get intimate before marriage. She believes in spirituality and true love without physical intimacy and being loyal towards each other. Sunaina never understand his desires and most of the time taken him for granted. In Delhi, Vinay met Megha in his MBBS College. She has recently broke up with her ex-boyfriend and is really upset and mentally unstable. Vinay is helping her in coping up with her break up and they both started liking each other. One day he got the chance to propose her and which she also accepted. Megha was doing every possible things to maintain her new chemistry with Vinay and she wants to win his heart by any means. She was cooking for him, did his laundry, gifted him expensive things without any occasion, did physical intimacy to prove her love for him. In short, she does all whatever is possible to keep Vinay in her life forever. Vinay likes her devotion towards him but also can't forget Sunaina completely, so he had been keeping relation with both the girls until get caught. And this continues for six months but one day Megha caught him red handed and rang Sunaina and rest all we know. This incident changes Sunaina's behavior towards all males as she stops believing them and she even lost faith in all male even her male friends which keeps her upset all the time. She can't even focus in her career and all this continues for another six months. But life never stops for anybody and soon she realizes that she can't punish herself for other's fault. She is having few close friends who always tried to cheer up her and bring her out for parties, hangouts, shopping etc., so that she could forget Vinay and his deception. Even they introduced her to new guys so that she could forget Vinay and move on in her life and stop calling Vinay unnecessarily.

After eight months, Sunaina understood that she should move on and prioritize herself and so she has started taking self-care, self-pampering as her close friends told her to do. She knows that when she dressed up well and in good mood she looks prettier. To take first step in the direction of self-love, she has changed her old wardrobe with new colorful fun and stylish clothes for a fresh start and also meeting new people with a happy mask on her face. In few days, she excels in hiding her pain from others and not allowing anyone to enter her soul again. Her friends have decided to do group dating for her till she get a better partner or could recover her current situation. Group dating means when all the couple who are friends and will do dating together like a group hangout. Her best friends meet their boyfriends along with Sunaina and they date together. One fine day an army guy, Ashish, one of her friend's friend returned back home after completing his army training. He came to meet them where he met Sunaina. Ashish gets impressed by Sunaina's presence of humor, her appearance and her personality. He has started liking her and trying to talk to her privately. To get the opportunity to talk to her separately to know about her more, Ashish throw a grand party for name sake of new job as Lt. Col. Sunaina and her friends are being invited in this grand party. As now Sunaina wants to move on and enjoy her life to the fullest, so she gets ready to go to the party and picked a red gown from the shop with matching stilettoes for the party. She is more confident now because she knows she will look stunning in that party. Ashish who was already impressed by her personality, now also gets mesmerized by her beauty. He has started conversation with her like a gentleman. He is continuously praising her and trying to impress her in all the possible ways. Sunaina understood his intensions but pretending as if she doesn't know anything. She is enjoying all the attentions getting from him. Finally Ashish asked her to dance with him as all other couple are on the dance floor. She agreed to dance with him and after long time Sunaina seems happy so all her friends in that party are also happy and excited except one and that is Riya's boyfriend, Sohail.

From last two years, he was in love with Sunaina but couldn't express his feelings to her because she is a close friend of Riya and Sunaina was in relationship with Vinay. But after their break up, Sohail thought of proposing her and leave Riya.

Riya is dominating in nature and belongs to some different rituals. As per Sohail, he was doing compromise and sacrifice with her. Riya and Sohail are of completely different mindset and most of the time she forced him to follow her decisions. Sohail cares for Riya but due to her stubborn nature, their relationship gets bitter day by day. On the other hand Sunaina is more understanding, caring, beautiful yet no ego kind of girl.

In party while dancing, Ashish started chatting with Sunaina asking about her future plans, family background, her dreams, her relationship status and everything. Sunaina replied all his queries even told him that she wants to do job after marriage and become financially independent. She also told him all the truth about her past that she had an ex-boyfriend and their relationship ends up in a bitter note. Ashish likes her honesty and proposes her while dancing. He bent on his knees and proposes her for marriage. Sunaina refuses his proposal and told him that she doesn't believe any guy and so she don't want to get into any relationship. Ashish keeps on trying to convince her that all guys are not the same and told her that he will take care of her always and being loyal to her. Sunaina likes the attention she is getting from Ashish but she can't forget Vinay's disloyalty so she refuses him again. But after that party, she keeps on chatting with him because it diverts her mind from all her sufferings. She also told Ashish that now she wants to focus only in her career and upcoming entrance exams. Ashish's heart breaks with her rejection but still he have hope that she will accept him one day. Sunaina keeps talking to Ashish as a friend and Sunaina's friends are happy as they noticed improvements in her behavior. She became more focused, career oriented, happier than before. She wrapped up herself and slowly and slowly moved on from her past experiences. She promised herself not to fall in love anymore with any guy again but life has some other plans decided for her.

One day Riya's boyfriend, Sohail called up Sunaina and request her to meet him in a café as he needs to discuss something very important with her. As Sunaina was thinking of going out for long to get a break from her exam pressure, so she agreed to meet him in a cafe. Since two months, she is being preparing for her upcoming exams without any distractions, so she is thinking of taking one day break from books. As she is going out after long time so she takes time and dressed up well to feel self-good. She wears a *chickankari* white *kurti* with a pair of denim, *mojris* and *jhumkas* simply to pamper herself and not to impress anyone. When she reached café where Sohail requested her to meet, she saw him already waiting there for her, wearing a white tee shirt and a pair of decent blue denim and new white sneakers. In past, Sohail never wear sneakers, in fact, he doesn't like to wear Sneaker. He was always in pair of *chappals* even when dating with Riya. For the first time in his life, he dressed up to impress her.

He welcomed her with red rose's bouquet and walk along with her to their reserved seat in that cafe. He has shown all courtesy like pulling chair for her and make her sit comfortably. Sunaina is little amazed by his change in behavior but not telling him anything as she wants to know the matter for which he called her in that café. After few minutes she asked him eagerly, *"what happened Sohail? Why did you called me like this?* Sohail replied, *"Please have patience Sunaina."* Then he called the waiter and ordered all her favorite foods. She gets more surprised by his mysterious behavior. Earlier when all of them hangout together, eat together, Sohail had noticed her, what she eats, what she likes so he knows what she likes to eat. Without noticing his efforts to impress her, unknowingly, she keeps on asking him with a curiosity on her face. He keeps on changing the topic and has started complimenting her, *"You are looking more beautiful today like a fairy on the earth."*

She laughs louder and replied, *"stop flirting or else I will tell everything to Riya."* Sohail replied, *"why are you talking about Riya, it's us only you and me."* Sunaina replied, because she is your girlfriend and she have all the rights to know all your activities. Sohail has assembled courage and finally holds her hand while staring at her eyes and told her that he don't love Riya rather he loves her from last two years. He couldn't tell her about his feelings earlier because she was in a relationship at that time.

Sunaina's eyes gets filled with tears because she is recalling her past again, how Vinay had cheated her and fooling two girls at the same time and cheated both of them. She doesn't want to repeat the same situation again in her life. And also she don't want to break Riya's trust. So she left the café immediately. Sohail called her repeatedly but she didn't listen to him and even ignored his phone calls too. After three to four hours and 60-70 miscalls, she picked up the phone. Sohail asked her, *"Why you left me like this? It's breaking me from inside and I love you a lot."* Sunaina replied, *"Then what about Riya? Why you are thinking of leaving her. She is your girlfriend from past 2 years."*

He replied that he is not happy with her, she is dominating in nature and she is not his type of girl. He told her *"Rather, you are my type of girl and my first choice, I can leave her for you"*. Sunaina replied, *"If today you can leave her for me, tomorrow you will leave me for someone else"*. She also told him that right now she don't want to get into any love relationship with anyone and also she do not want to distract from her dreams and career. She also told him that she wants to crack the upcoming entrance exam anyhow and get admission in some professional college. Sohail replied that he will be waiting for her always and hung up the call. Sohail felts disheartened but still have hope that she will came back one day. Later on Sohail has done break up with Riya and told her all the truth. Riya felts humiliated and stop talking to both Sohail and Sunaina.

Sunaina has written all possible entrance exams for both medical and engineering. She has been worshiping all religion gods and visited almost all worship places wherever people had suggested her. This time she was so desperate to achieve her goal that no one could resist her. In the mid of that year, her entrance exam results are out and finally she has cleared the engineering entrance exam and got admission in a renowned engineering college at Chennai which is almost 2634 km far away from her native place.

LoveNote : Some cheats because of circumstances, some to escape from commitment, some to get better life partner, it's never your fault if somebody cheats you. Most of the time it's the circumstances. Flirt is when someone fall for your words, lust is when someone fall for your beauty and love is when someone fall for your soul.

Girlfriend should be more beautiful than her Boyfriend

Sunaina is excited for her new beginning. She is being engaged in shopping along with her mother. She has bought her new college outfits and all other hostel necessities. After getting admission in engineering college, she gets back her lost confidence and respect in her family. She is feeling out of the world now and not recalling any of her past sorrows and worst memories with Vinay. All her family members and friends are being wishing and gifting her for her new beginning. Before going to Chennai she has planned to meet all her close friends except Riya and Sohail. Among all close friends, Sunaina have two besties Neelam and Aisha who are special for her. She meet both of them together so that they can chill out, share secrets and discuss their future plans.

The day before they meet, Aisha went to her cousin brother, Shaheed's home and gets impressed of his achievements. Next day when she meet them, she keeps on flaunting about her brother Shaheed in front of them without any reason. She told them that her brother won Mr. handsome tag in inter College and state level competition. Along with good looks, he is a MBA topper and a down to earth person. He had never proposed any girl in his entire life rather girls are proposing him always because he is decent and cute and have strong built physique too. He used to go gym every day and maintain his physique so well that he is not only popular among girl's even guys also admires him. Neelam and Sunaina makes fun of Aisha and told her that what she is saying is all her misconception because at current generation, no one is like that.

After hearing their words, Aisha challenged both Neelam and Sunaina that if they meet her brother and make him bound to propose one of them she will give anything they want. In addition to that she also told whenever they will meet him, maximum chances is that they will get crush on him. Neelam gets irritated and accepted the challenge to break Aisha's misconception about her brother. She convinced Sunaina also to accept her challenge to prove that all the guys are same and her brother is not an exception. This challenge is going to be a turning point in Sunaina's life which will change her life completely in future.

Neelam and Aisha has invited Aisha's brother Shaheed for a movie together and also convinced Sunaina to join them for the last time before going to Chennai. Shaheed reached movie hall ten minutes before time along with his two friends. Neelam and Sunaina planned to wear short skirt and mini dress with stilettoes to prove Aisha that his brother is also like other guys. Movie tickets and foods are already booked by Shaheed for six of them to watch the latest movie together. As he knows very well that this will be the first impression on both Sunaina and Neelam. When they meet at movie hall, Shaheed gets impressed by Sunaina's savage beauty and down to earth nature. Shaheed behaves like a decent man as he knows very well how to impress any girl. Neelam, Aisha and Shaheed's friend exchange their numbers while watching movie. Shaheed got Sunaina's phone number from her sister but he never called her as he knows that girls don't like clingy guys. One week later, six of them again meet in a café and this time Sunaina also finds interest on Shaheed because after getting so many opportunities still he is not flirting with any of them. Whenever they meet, he talks about passion, career, respecting women, social issues, independent women, etc. She feels delighted to talk to him and also shared her future plans. She told him that she will do job in future and want to be financially independent as her mother wants her to be an independent career woman. Shaheed cheers her up for her determination and encourage her to follow her dreams. He also clarified her that he likes working women and in future he will *allow his wife* to do job. Sunaina gets confidence from his words and from then, they started dating each other in cafes and parks discussing their future plans. But still Shaheed has not shown his *flirting skills* to her, instead he shows over caring and protectiveness towards her which is being slowly healing her past wounds. Before going to Chennai, they meet again. On that day, Shaheed has admitted in front of Neelam and Aisha that he likes Sunaina but can't say in front of her. Neelam gets excited when heard this as she wins the bet with Aisha. When Neelam told this to Sunaina, she also gets into dilemma as she has started liking him and his behavior towards her but in few days she has to move to the other state for further studies and she will be unable to meet him again.

Finally the day arrived when Sunaina has to fly to Chennai to start her new endeavor. That day, Shaheed breaks his silence and proposed her at the airport. He requested her to take time to decide and not to reply in hurry as he is not expecting any reply from her. He told her that he will wait his whole life for her. Actually he already knows about her past from his sister, Aisha. And he also knows that there are maximum chances of rejection from her. Sunaina is in dilemma and so without replying anything, she moved to Chennai.

Sunaina wants to fulfill her mother's dream of getting a degree and then a decent job. Sunaina's mom is a home maker but she wants her daughter to be financially independent. Sunaina always remind herself what her mother has told her to do.

First day in college and Sunaina seems very excited. She gets up early, dressed up in new clothes that she bought in native and stepped forward to her 1st class in engineering college. She is scared of getting ragged by seniors when she enter the college. At the same time, she is consoling herself that she is a brave girl who had faced a lot recently, a heart break, cheater boyfriend, an academic failure, family disgrace, shattering of self-confidence and coped up with all but never afraid, cracks toughest engineering entrance exam with all such bad circumstances. She is self-encouraging and self-consoling that ragging is just a silly, stupid thing as compared to her past experiences. With such mix feelings when she has entered the college, she saw a huge Ganesh idol is there at the college entrance. As she worships and believes in Lord Ganesh, a Hindu god, so when she saw the idol, she gets confidence from within that everything will be alright here. Now with positive hope, she moved forward towards her department. While moving towards her department, she saw other departments like Mechanical, Electrical, Aeronautics and Computer Science and as we all know in India, Engineering colleges means all boys students, ratio will be like 100 male students per female engineering student. However Sunaina has already prepared her mind for all such things. Like other Engineer girl students, she also knows that she will be eve teased by many. To avoid these, she is walking faster than usual and not doing any eye contact with anyone and her face either towards downward or looking straight as she is pretending to ignore all such shouts of her name by college boys. She is bit surprised also that how could they all knew her name, she came here for the first time. Engineering guys are the real "jugadus" in the world. Nothing is impossible for them if they want anything then they will do it anyhow by hook or by crook. They arranged her complete bio-data from the admission cell from where they got her mobile number.

Though many students' keeps on teasing her, few are singing songs, some are calling her name, calling by color that she wore, among those students, a simple sweet guy who is neither teasing nor making her uncomfortable, rather stopping others from teasing a new girl.

When these guys are not listening to him and teasing her non-stop, Sunaina gets irritated and stop walking, looked up and searching the guy who called her by her name to scold him but she didn't find anyone in the huge crowd standing on the balcony and stairs. And that sweet guy is simply staring at her with blank head and simply praising her simplicity, her almond kohl eyes her natural pink lips. He is admiring her as she looks different from crowd, wearing white translucent *chickankari kurti* with a pair of denim and printed bag and *mojris*. After a minute, Sunaina left the place as she can't find anyone to scold.

Unfortunately in Sunaina's class there are out of eighty five students only five are girls including Sunaina and rest all are guys. These kind of inappropriate gender ratio is new for her as she had studied in co-ed schools where there is usually almost equal no of boys and girls. It's a bit awkward for any female who has entered an engineering college for the first time because still our society has considered engineering is for boys and mostly engineering colleges are male dominant place.

Sunaina is a meritorious student but she loves to sit on backbenches as she finds it cool but in engineering college, she has intentionally choose first bench to sit because most of the class is occupied by tall, huge guys and it will be difficult for her to see the board and also to get faculty's attention. Sunaina sit with a girl from Bengaluru, name Stuthi and trying to start conversation with her so that she can make her first friend in this college.

Sunaina is sharing her views, her likes and dislikes with Stuthi and vice versa. They both find each other interesting and opposite in nature. Stuthi is studious, sincere, overall looks edgy, smart, slim, short heighted, straight hair, cute face, small eyes, milky white skin tone and simply looks like a doll while Sunaina is taller than her but healthier than Stuthi, big almond eyes, attractive face features and have charismatic personality. Sunaina is also meritorious and studious but she don't want to show off her studious side to anyone as she thought that studious persons are judged as boring and she never want that tag for herself. She wants to be popular and influence others. Generally she studies secretly after mid night when all fell asleep and during day hours, she shows her damn care attitude towards studies and exams. Though she gets rank among topper in her class, some of her classmates gets jealous and some are curious about her nature which increases her popularity among them. In few months, she has achieved the fame and popularity in entire college as few talks about her style, few about her rank and marks without studying and few thought that she is damn rich so she might be buying her marks with money while other thought that professor gives her more marks because she is pretty. All these rumors has been spread about her in entire college. On the contrary, Stuthi shows what she is, a sincere, studious girl but sometimes she is also competing with Sunaina and most of the time they got equal marks which irritates her more. Sunaina has good observing ability so she understands other's mind towards her and also she could read Stuthi's mind too but still never tried to change herself. Although she have lots of friends in college and hostel as she knows how to maintain friendship and do all possible help to her friends. All these things increases Sunaina's popularity among both students and professors. Everyone likes her and some of them wanted to get her as girlfriend or life partner.

Suddenly one day Sunaina got a call from some unknown guy, asking her name and random questions. Earlier also she got calls like these and by the way which is common in any engineering college but this call is different from them because it's not from any student but from a newly joined professor and ex- student of the same college. After getting few blank calls Sunaina has ignored the calls and blocked the number. After some time, she gets another call from some random number and she has blocked that number too.

Sunaina & Stuthi both were facing difficulties over there due to ragging by their seniors in college and hostels but still they are bravely handling everyday chaos without effecting their studies. With passing time both of them became best friends and developed a strong bond of faith, trust, care and protectiveness. They both like each other's company so much that they forget there are eighty boys and three other girls in their classroom. They have taken care of each and every issues together and if required, they fights for each other. They have started enjoying little things together and creating memories forever. Sunaina and Stuthi spends all their festivals together and did their first rain dance together. Together they learn how to cook Maggi, coffee, sandwich. They do shopping and movies only with each other and also saving each other from hostel warden, hiding food from the mess for each other, sharing clothes and all essential things together.

One day Stuthi shares Sunaina about her new crush Sujoy and tell her how wonderful person he is. They have everything common in them and both love each other's company a lot. After hearing these from Stuthi, Sunaina feels insecure but she hides her emotions from her. After getting confirmation from Sunaina, Stuthi has started dating Sujoy and now she is spending most of her time with him either on call or on date. During lunch time also Stuthi is going to canteen with him. She has started going for shopping, eating street food, movies, parties with Sujoy only and most of the time engaged with him on phone. After few months, Sunaina has started feeling left out and lonely. Because of Stuthi she has not make any other friends. And now when Stuthi is not giving her time and so she is feeling lonely, upset and scared of loosing her one and only friend in the college. Sunaina has started calling Shaheed to divert her mind from her friend Stuthi. Now whenever she feels lonely, she does texting and calling Shaheed.

When Sunaina told Stuthi about her insecurities to loose their friendship, Stuthi laughs at her and tell her to talk to Shaheed and also advised her that she shouldn't lose a person like Shaheed. She also told her that she will not get a guy with such combination of handsomeness and decency. Shaheed is a gym freak and most of the girls are attracted by his gentleman like polished behavior with well-built physique, 5'10" tall, copper tan skin tone, edgy face features and strong built arms. Shaheed behaves *extra polite and decent* with girls. With passing days Sunaina has also started believing him. She slowly and slowly gets influenced by her friend and decided to give him a chance to enter in her life. Now Shaheed has calling her every single day and text her every single hour and unknowingly he is leaving impact on her and *intentionally trying to be her daily habit* which is a red flag *when done intentionally.* Sunaina finds her day incomplete without talking to him. This continues for almost three months and suddenly one day Shaheed called her to tell her that he is in Chennai to meet her and standing in front of her college gate. By hearing these, Sunaina gets shocked and run towards the college gate. When she have seen him right there standing in front of her college gate, her tears rolled down and she stand in awe. She feels both delighted and stressed. She feels delighted because still there is someone who cares for her and also stressed because she don't want any unnecessary drama in front of her college.

She run to him and says hello to him and took him to her college canteen to avoid any awkward situation in front of her college entrance and also she wants to talk privately. With stress on her face, she asked him that why he came all of sudden without informing. He replied her that he wanted to do job there in Chennai so that he can see and meet her anytime. She told him that she can't meet him anytime but sometimes they may meet. Then he is requesting her to help him in getting job there. She agreed to help him in getting job. She is happy to see him but she is confused to get into any relationship at present. She wants to focus in her career first.

Sunaina has been requesting all of her male friends for his stay and finally arranged one for him. She has also requested Stuthi's boyfriend for his job. On the contrary, Shaheed's only intention is to impress Sunaina and make her fall for his love because Sunaina is the only girl who didn't accept him and impressed by his personality. *He can't handle this rejection so he tried his level best to get her in his trap*.

Sunaina asked help from Sujoy as he is working in a reputed IT MNC. Sunaina brought him to meet her friend

Stuthi and her boyfriend Sujoy regarding his job interviews. Stuthi was already fond of Shaheed, his looks and his extra polite & decent behavior. To make Shaheed comfortable among them, Stuthi initiates talk with him and has given order *(in fun ways)* to her boyfriend to help him out anyhow. She actually wants to see her friend Sunaina happy and settled. But her friendly behavior and helping nature is misinterpreted by Shaheed. When Stuthi and Sujoy left the place, Shaheed told Sunaina that her friend Stuthi was continuously flirting with him and she was not a trust worthy friend of her. By ignoring his words, Sunaina told him to concentrate on his lined up interviews arranged by Sujoy. Shaheed has played the same game with all of her close friends from college and school. He told the same thing even for Sunaina's sister but Sunaina keeps on ignoring all these red flags. In the name of interviews, he asked monetary help from Sunaina and promised her to return all when he get his first salary. Sunaina keeps on helping him sometimes from her monthly expenses and the other time from her college semester fees. One day Shaheed told her that he got a job in a bank and for that he needs some twenty five thousand rupees for security deposit. Sunaina being a generous and kind hearted person, she gives him money from her college fees which if not paid on time to the college, she knows she have to pay penalty, but then also she helped him with twenty five thousand rupees. After one month, she get to know that it was a scam and all the money gets wasted. So she gets angry on Shaheed and asked her money back from him or else she will asked from his parents. After these Shaheed has started searching job seriously and within fifteen days he got a job and after one month when he gets his first salary then he brought Sunaina for treat and gifted her an AD jewelry set but *not returned her money back* which was comparatively a higher amount. Sunaina is happy and so again ignored another red flag. The very next day Shaheed has proposed Sunaina again and as usual she replied that let her focus on her studies for time being. But now scenarios are little different, he *show-off being* more responsible and caring towards her and becoming her daily habit. Now she has also started liking him because he is consistently loving her and waiting for her commitment.

After few months, one day when Sunaina is feeling low and lonely, coincidently Shaheed called her and she has started crying in front of him. Shaheed got the chance and indirectly proposes her and promised her that he will never let her cry again. He will do all efforts to make her happy and comfortable. As Sunaina is already in her weaker state of mind, without understanding anything she has committed to Shaheed. Now Shaheed knows all her weak points and strengths, so strategically he has started showing her extra pampering and possessiveness. He has started to pick up and drop her from college to hostel and hostel to college so that no other guys get chance to talk to her. He has also started controlling her from going to her friend's parties and college parties. If she wants to go then he will go along with her to these parties and she should be always with him. Wherever she goes whether it's shopping or eat-outs, he will go with her and started manipulating her mind against her friends that they are not trust worthy. He has been controlling her mind by saying that only he is her well-wisher and not anyone else. He has even started selecting her outfits what she should wear and what not to wear. He told her that modern day's outfits are for characterless women and not for her. Women looks beautiful only when they wear covered clothes and cover their head with scarfs. He also washed her brain by saying that women shouldn't talk to all guys if they are committed, if they do so other guys will judge their character. As per his opinion, man can do extra marital affairs but women can't because people will not judge a man but they will definitely judge a women's character. He does emotional blackmailing to do what he likes and keeps on calling her so that she will not get chance to interact with her friends and even family members. His intention is to make her isolated from everything that she loves. Like a slow poison he started demoralizing her and breaking her self- confidence by saying that she is not beautiful as earlier, her friends are prettier than her. He told her to wear fully covered salwar suit(clothes) because she don't look good in jeans and dresses and on the same time he told her that she looks like an aunty. He also tries to make her jealous by telling that her friends are admiring him a lot and she is lucky to have a loyal and handsome boyfriend like him. Sunaina has started believing these because she has also heard the same thing from her friends and sister as they had seen his good side only. He has also started praising other girls in front of her and makes her feel like she is an ordinary and less attractive girl by comparing her with her friends and random girls in public places. Her mind gets stuck and stops thinking what is right and what is wrong. She is so much in control of him that she dressed up according to him and does only those things that he likes. Anybody who losses his/ her freedom to think and express self will be lacking in self-confidence and never feel good about self. To control her mind, Shaheed does all possible ways like body shaming, comparing her to other beautiful girls and always pointing out her fault and praising her in front of her friend and sister so that he can show his favor to her. He is treating her like a puppet and all the time let her realize that he is doing favor to her.

Shaheed has also tried to spoil her friendship with Stuthi and her old friends. He told Stuthi that Sunaina does not trust her friendship and doubted her that she have an affair with him. For getting her sympathy, he told her that Sunaina is a different person now, she always fight with him and doesn't value his care for her. He tried the same trick even with Sunaina's sister and almost get succeeded in ruining all her close relationships whom she loves. He has even makes her against her parents, so that slowly and slowly she get cut off from them too. He had got succeeded in his plan of breaking her all relationships. But evil thought has a very short life span and so Shaheed did mistake. He has tried the same trick to her old school friend Neelam which is his biggest mistake ever and he fails utterly collapsed. After getting call from Shaheed and telling her that Sunaina is bitching about her and she is not trust-worthy, Neelam has scolded him back and immediately called Sunaina to tell her the whole incident and finally it has opened the blind-folds from her eyes. Now she could relate all the stuffs happened in the past and he was playing with her emotions and did tricks to control her mind completely. Then she has also realized that he had even stolen money many times from her debit cards which she was managing by asking from her parents. She has immediately checked her bank statement and found that whenever she has asked him to get money from ATM, he has always stolen some lump sum amount because generally we remember the first two figure and not the rest. She has also realized that she is in a trap now and to get out of it and her current situation, she has to get rid of him first but she have no idea how to do that. Except Neelam, all her friend circle knows that Shaheed is a very genuine guy, kind hearted, soft spoken, lovable person and if she left him then everyone will only blame her and she doesn't have that courage to face it.

Fortunately, one day Sunaina caught him red handed, she heard him saying "*I love you sweetheart*" to someone else in phone. Shaheed was in bathroom and talking to another girl and all of sudden Sunaina reached there and heard all his conversation with that girl from outside the bathroom door. She gets shocked for a while but this time she doesn't breakdown like earlier instead she has started shouting on him and scolding him loudly and telling him that she will not be with him anymore. She has also told him that she is fed up with this relationship and wanted to do break up with him. She has also told him not to show his face again. On that day she behaves absolutely opposite to her calm and vulnerable nature. Sunaina's behavior shows it clearly that she is done with this relationship and don't want to look back while Shaheed gets shocked by Sunaina's vigorous behavior. Shaheed has heights of confidence that after all such things happened then also he could manipulate her mind, convince her and manage the current situation. He thought that this time also he could convince her by his emotional blackmailing. So he has gone to the kitchen and take a knife in his hand and has started blackmailing her that he will cut his veins if she will left him. While Sunaina is determined this time that she will leave him permanently and don't want to see him again. She is pretending of not listening to his words and get up to go out of Sujoy's apartment as Shaheed is temporarily staying with him. To prove himself right, Shaheed hold the knife in his hand and started begging her to not leave him like this otherwise he will cut his veins. Sunaina gets angrier by his blackmailing behavior and tried to snatch the knife from his hand and saying him that she will not get affected by all these fake dramas, and if he needs then she will help him in cutting his veins. While snatching the knife from his hand, she did not realized that his palm gets cut by the knife and its bleeding heavily. In the meantime, Sujoy and Stuthi reached there in the apartment. They saw spots of blood everywhere on the floor and wall. Sujoy and Stuthi gets angry by their misconduct and told Shaheed to go out of their apartment immediately. Sunaina feels scared as his hand is bleeding continuously. She took him to the hospital and get bandaged his hand. He thought that this will definitely melt Sunaina's heart for him. But Sunaina didn't give a damn to him and comes out of the hospital, booked an auto-rickshaw and came back to her hostel. That day she cried a lot but not for being cheated again. She cried because how she was fooled by him and ignoring so many red flags in her relationship just to be with such a jerk for no reason.

She cried whole night but in the morning she wake up like a free bird after a long prison. She feels breathable now and her mind has started thinking again which was stuck earlier.

On the other side Shaheed was calling her non-stop since last evening incident but she didn't picked up his call rather blocked his calls and also block him from all her social media accounts. She was extremely frustrated from him and after so long, she feels confident and beautiful again like earlier.

She understands that beauty is nothing but what you feel about yourself from within. One can make it or break it by allowing others to appreciate or demoralize themselves. When she was with Shaheed, she had never felt beautiful which causes lacking in self- confidence but after break-up, she feels free and her confidence returns back. Now she could wear whatever she likes and meet her friends again so that she can clear all misunderstandings between them which were created by Shaheed.

She called her old school friend Neelam to thank her for saving her life and for believing her. She had called Aisha also but Aisha took her brother's side and try to convince her not to do break up with him. She tried to convince her that in every relationship such silly mistakes may happen but one shouldn't break their relation for such small reasons. As a close friend she should take her side but she was taking her brother's side and was telling her that Shaheed is a genuine guy and he loves her a lot. He will never cheat her for any random girl. He was talking to that girl because he was under pressure of that girl who was blackmailing him to love her and be with her. Sunaina had already make up her mind and don't want to return to her misery life again. She understood that Aisha will never acknowledged her situation so she has stopped talking to Aisha.

Now Sunaina has finally started taking care of herself both mentally and physically. She called her close friends and relatives whom she was unable to talk and meet because of him.

Now she can realized that how Shaheed had ruined her life mentally, physically, financially and with her close friends and family members. And he had actually make her look older than her age. As she was a student of 21 years but due to his mental harassment she had lost her youthfulness, freedom to laugh loudly, freedom to think and it was like a golden heart shaped cage where one couldn't live her life freely. The strongest support of a child is his/her parents and Shaheed had intentionally destroyed her support first so that if she feels alone then she have only one option and that is Shaheed. She had also realized that he had always telling her that he made her beautiful and taught her dressing sense but when he was walking on street with her then he was checking out only those girls who were in short dresses. She called her parents and Stuthi and told them everything happened with her. Now Shaheed was fully exposed in front of all. Shaheed had returned back to his hometown and played another game to destroy her. He along with his friend had gone to meet her parents to tell them that Sunaina is his wife and they are already married. Now he came to know that she had not tell her parents so he came to inform them. He had also warned them that they shouldn't force her to marry anyone else.

As Sunaina had already informed everything to them, so they knew that this guy is lying. After hearing all his nonsense, Sunaina's parent threatened him and his friend that if they will not go out of their house then forcefully they have to call police. After hearing this from them, he understood that he is failed again.

Like earlier, Sunaina has not compromised with her studies and cleared all her six semester exams without any back papers. Now she is in final year and promised herself that she will not do such mistakes again. Her all these past sufferings become life lessons for her. Everyone on this planet have faced some incidents in their life and those incidents become lessons for their entire life but few people have more such chapters in their life. Life taught them complete guide of such lessons for their betterment. And these lessons makes one stronger version of themselves.

After five break ups, she is totally changed to a new version. She became more confident than before and has stopped taking shit of others. Now she doesn't allow anyone to demoralize, dominate and control her. She has started doing whatever she thinks right. Now if anyone tried to control or demoralize her then she strictly told them that she couldn't change herself and will remain the same, if possible be with her and if not then free to go away from her. She had stopped regretting her past rather she is proud that she could escaped from that trap. She is motivated towards self-loving and self-pampering. She has started praising herself every day in front of the mirror. She slammed those who does body shamming. Now she got her mental peace back and confidence to the next level. Her friends and family members are astonished by her new behavior and confidence level and realized that she became a totally different person.

Love Note: Beauty is something which has no benchmark and can't define in words. If someone is beautiful for one, might be not for the others. But confident people always look beautiful and stand out from crowd. People see you the way you convey yourself. So first raise your self-esteem up and then expect respect and admiration from others. Before every break ups, all get some red flags which unfortunately most of the time get ignored. So one should be alert at the first red flag and without informing anything one should observe his/her partner if further red flags are there or not. And most important is not to change yourself for anyone because losing originality will not last longer. And if someone loves you, then he/she will love the way you are without changing you.

Love, Affection and Attraction

Sunaina had completed her all seven semesters with excellent grades despite all the troubles and now she is in her final semester. But Sunaina's life lessons not yet finished. Some more difficulties are waiting in her upcoming days. As God wants to give her something very precious so given her more chapters to overcome. She is now more confident than before so hopefully can handle upcoming worst situations better than before.

While she is busy in preparing for her final semester project and assignments, she got to know that their current Environmental subject professor has resigned and will be replaced by a young professor. Do you remember the young lecturer who used to call her while she was a fresher? That young lecturer is now become a senior professor and is going to replace her subject teacher. This professor was liking Sunaina from her first day in college. Earlier he had arranged her mobile no from his students to propose her. After that incident Sunaina had blocked his number and changed her phone number. That professor had few senior class friends whom he had shared her number. They also called her to chat, to propose and to disturb unnecessarily.

She escaped that time by changing her mobile number but this time she is not that lucky. In final semester, these professor had got all the right to deduct her marks in assignments and exams. All engineering exams are divided into two parts – written exam and viva/assignment in which she has to appear physically for the test/assignments which covers almost 1/3rd of the total marks and rest from the written exam. That professor has taken it as opportunity to talk to her again and this time being a professor, he could call her anytime. Sunaina understands everything and so she always tried to avoid him and reply rudely whenever he tried to talk to her personally. She knows very well that if she give him opportunity to do personnel talk then he may propose her and as a subject professor she couldn't avoid him or complaint against him to the management. She understood the importance of final semester exam so she didn't want to create any hurdle to her exams. She also thought that only few months left for the final exam and till then she have to avoid him and after getting degree no one could damage her career. Whenever she saw that professor is coming towards her, she changed her route. After so much efforts one day that professor got chance to talk to her and expressed his feelings in front of her. He told her that he liked her from the first day he saw her and tried to talk to her many times. He had requested her to accept his proposal or else he will not pass her in exams. He has threatened her that she will get zero marks in his subject if she rejects his proposal. But Sunaina with full confidence refused his proposal on the spot and tell him that she couldn't think of loving him. She also told him that she respects teachers and professor but couldn't mix it with other feelings. In her mind she had decided that she will lose 1/3rd marks which comes from viva/assignments and will cover rest of the $2/3^{rd}$ marks from written test which is not controlled by him and will be checked by the other board people. Professor felts offended by her reply and again threatened her that he will do anything to make her fail and not get the engineering degree. She has also challenged him that she will pass and score highest marks in all subjects no matter whether he will support or not. She told him that if he will still trouble her then she will put complaint against him to the college management and he will lose his job. That professor has not taken her seriously and continued bothering her. Then Sunaina has decided to punish him for his misbehavior and put a complaint of harassment against him. It's unbelievable for that professor and hard to digest that a weak, soft spoken student like her can take such a daring step. This is beyond his imagination.

After these incident, Sunaina get a tag in her college as "*heart breaker machine*". Earlier she was extra emotional and one who cares other's feeling. She was soft in nature and can't refuse or say no to anyone. Earlier while taking decision, she kept other's opinion on priority though she was disagreed so that the other person shouldn't get hurt. But now she is completely opposite to her nature which is indigestible for many students in the college.

College Management team has taken strict action against that professor and rusticate him for six months. That professor said sorry to her in front of everyone and promised her that he will not do it again. Management has appointed another professor for class and added a new rule for all professors that if anybody will do such kind of blackmailing to any students, they will immediately loose their job and may be put them behind the bars in case of harassment.

Love Note: One should know how to distinguish between love, affection and attraction and shouldn't destroy their life in such unnecessary distractions. One should learn how to say no boldly to anyone if they are in such awkward situations. Have faith in yourself and always fight for what is right. Love is something pure and nowadays people are taking wrong route to get their love which is actually for accomplishing their desire and ego and definitely not for love.

Ideal Age for Love

Sunaina, one day, sitting in her hostel balcony with her room mates. Suddenly one of her roommate has shouted from inside that "*Vinay is calling you n number of times, pick up the phone buddy*". Sunaina gets astonished by hearing this. She thought that might be she heard Vinay by mistake instead of some other name. Though she run inside to pick up the phone and see there are 56 miscalls from Vinay. She has checked the number twice whether its Vinay's number or not and after confirming she thought for a while that she will not call him back as she is being afraid of getting weak in front of him and currently she does not want to show her weakness to him. But she wants to know the reason of his call so she has taken a deep breath and gathered courage to call him back. When she called him, within a second Vinay has attended her call and greet hello with a very low voice. He asked her how is she and what is she doing now? Sunaina gets shocked by his changed behavior. He pretends like nothing happened between them. She thought in her mind that how shameless he is and why she had wasted her time with him and sacrificed career. She is questioning herself that why she even cried for him? He was not that worthy. After a while, Vinay asked, "*Are you there? How are you?*" She replied that she is doing well. He asked, "*How's life going on*?" She simply replied fantastic.

He asked, *"Are you angry with me yet?"* She replied that she is not angry at all and actually she forgets everything. He asked, *"Then why are you not talking properly, is anyone with you?"* She replied that no one is there with her and this is the only way she speaks and if he doesn't like then he is allowed to drop the call. Vinay replied, *"I like all your ways of speaking because I always like you."* Sunaina asked him that whether he called her to talk this unnecessary things? Vinay replied, *"No Sunaina, actually I want to say you that I love you and will always love you and no matter you forgive me or not but I am still waiting for you."* Sunaina replied boldly that after so many years, all his words are meaningless to her and she doesn't like him anymore and will never like him again. He requested her that they could be friends at least. He told her what he thought that she has neither forgave him nor moved on and still there is love in her heart for him. He told that he has been calling her several times in last year but couldn't find her correct number. Once he got her number but within a month it was changed. He told her that because she had often changed her mobile number so he couldn't contact her before. He is talking non-stop about his feelings for her and now he has started explaining why he had to left her. The day when they had their last conversation over phone, on that day he had a fight with Megha and after that their relationship was getting worse day by day. They both loose faith on each other. She had started cheating on him. He told Sunaina that Megha was not as loyal as her. Megha was dating another guy also which she was hiding from him. He told that they had mutually break up within a month after that fight. And after that he had tried calling her several times but couldn't talk. He also praised her by saying that he was immature at that time so he had lost a girl like her and she was a precious gift of god to him which he lost due to his stupidity. He has requested her to forgive him for all this. He also praised her by saying that Megha was not a marriage type girl and no one wants to marry such a girl. She had no comparison with you and you are everybody's dream girl whom one wants to marry. But he realized it lately and till he understood this she had already shifted to another place. After hearing all this explanation Sunaina replied, "*Yes you have realized it very late*". He asked why with curiosity. And also asked her that does she have any boyfriend now? She replied, *"No, I don't have but I don't want any more nonsense in my life and don't need stupid jerks for love."*

He asked with anger, "*what do you mean? Why do you used such words and why are you so much changed?*" She replied "*All thanks to you and with time now I am able to recognize persons like you. A blind person will loose his stick once and not always. I am loving this change what I am today. I don't need any boyfriend to support me as I am self-sufficient for myself.*" He told her that she has become stronger and bolder than before. He replied that he will wait if she wants to do a fresh start of their relationship. She replied him that she knows her strength and she doesn't want any fresh start. She told that the age when they met, both of them were immature teenager but she was loyal and had ethics and he was cheater and opportunist. And now when they are grown-up and in their early 20's, they both have learned lessons from their past due to which she became bold and stronger and he seems like weaker and looser. She told him that he had lost her forever on that day when he and Megha called her. She told that she wants him to regret for his entire life. She told that your bad karmas had taught me lessons and as she was innocent that time so on behalf of her, Karma had taken revenge from him. Sunaina told him that she is happier today and he seems upset and depressed. Sunaina also told, "*On that day you told me not to call you again and today Karma has given me the chance to say you the same, don't call me again. I don't want to talk to you anymore and not even want to see your face in my life again. This is our last call and lastly I want to thank you for all the worst lessons that you had taught me. Good Bye Forever!*" And she hung up the call and blocked him.

Love Note: There is no ideal age for love, it can happen at any age with anyone. But what matters is you and your behavior in that relationship during that age. No one can escape from Karma, I believe. Vinay gets punished for his Karma. His second girlfriend also did the same with him and neither Sunaina accept him again. If you loved anyone no matter what is your age, be loyal, devoted and trust-worthy in that relationship.

Love vs Money

Sunaina is now 22nd years old and her degree is about to be completed. Sunaina's relatives are suggesting her parents that they should start searching groom for her from now so that they will get a deserving groom within two years for her marriage. In the meantime, one of their family friend has brought a marriage proposal for Sunaina and their son, named Abhay Malhotra. He belongs to a rich business family and pursuing his Engineering from the same institute where Sunaina is doing her engineering. Abhay is a spoiled son of a rich dad. He took admission in engineering college through management quota. He spends a lot in branded clothes and showing off his father's wealth to everyone. He have his own three luxury cars and two super bikes. He spends money recklessly in alcohol, clubbing and pubbing. He is always surrounded with rich guys and girls. He have a long list of his ex-girlfriends.

Sunaina's parents wants her to meet Abhay because they know his parents and his family background. They want a good family and a settled life-partner for her. As a son of Mr. Malhotra, he will definitely join his father's business as CEO after graduation. Like any other concerned parents, Sunaina's parents also want a comfortable life for her. So they pressurized her to meet Abhay once. Her parents don't know about his bad habits. They only knows that he belongs to a familial rich and cultured family and future CEO of his dad's existing business. They thought that their daughter will get a happy life if she will marry him and became daughter in law of Malhotra family who are their close friends and have good fame in society. They know the Malhotra family as friend so they thought that their son should be the same as his father.

After non- stop convincing, Sunaina has agreed to meet Abhay. She told her mom that she had a very worst experience regarding boys and she can't tolerate any non-sense of any guy. Her mother told her that her love life never works because she had always chosen wrong persons in her life and so she should have faith in her parent's choice because they better knows what she want in actual. For second opinion, she has asked her roommate Ruhani. And Ruhani has also advised her to listen to her mother. She told her that they have more experience than us and also that they already know his parents. Ruhani forced her to meet Abhay and told her that the most important thing in marriage life is money and Abhay Malhotra is already a rich guy with a settled future. She has been teasing Sunaina that if she will not marry Abhay then Ruhani, herself will do. Ruhani tried to convince her by saying that she doesn't have to work 9-5 for money in future, she will have already that much money and she will be the next company CEO. If she marry him, she will have number of luxury cars, own driver, chef, helper and all that luxury things that any girl dream in her marriage life. After hearing all this, Sunaina asked her, *"And what about self-respect? My parents send me to this engineering college so that I will become financial Independent, self-sufficient and then only one can respect me."* Sunaina told her that she can't compromise with her self-respect. After so many heart breaks and hard times she get back her self- respect and now it's her first priority in life and for no one she could compromise it. Since her teenage time, she had fantasy to do a love marriage with someone like Raj from DDLJ who will transform her boring life to a happening and exciting life. She also thinks in her fantasy that if she get someone like him then she will take stand for her love and if required even against her elders too. Actually she was obsessed with love marriages shown by Bollywood industry and actually scared of marrying an unknown person as generally happens in arrange marriages. She was scared as if she marry someone whom she don't know then she have to spend her whole life with that stranger person without loving him and which was not acceptable by her at that time. But after facing so many heart breaks and cheaters, her opinion of marriage has changed and now she trust her parents that they will do better choice for her. She feels herself as failure in choosing partners and judging people. At present time her all teenage fantasy dreams had shuttered down. She had lost faith in love marriages. She thought that her parents did arrange marriage and they are still together and so she have finally decided to do arrange marriage like her parents.

Ruhani keeps on convincing her that if she will meet Abhay before marriage like dating then they will get time to understand each other and might be it will convert to a love cum arrange marriage. She has also confirmed her that in Abhay's case there will be no scary surprises because both their parents know each other very well which will be a positive sign for her. So by saying all these

Ruhani succeeded in convincing her and also told her that only few lucky girls can get such a rich and noble family. She told her that she don't have to suffer for anything in life. She can continue her career, have uncountable money, property, cars, branded clothes, etc. Sunaina is a bit confused but still doing what Ruhani has told her and agreed to meet him with a positive hope for a happy start. She thought that she had already so many worst experiences and she broke many times and stand again boldly so if this will also not work then also she can tackle it. She is in a mood of giving herself another chance to live a dream life.

Next day, Sunaina informed her parents that she is going to meet Abhay and asked them his number. Sunaina and Abhay's parents mutually decided a café for their first meeting and informed both of them. After so long Sunaina is getting ready again like before. She wear a blue ragged denim with a white casual tee-shirt. She had already decided that she will not go in traditional attire as her parents told her to do. Her hair tied on a high ponytail, a pair of hoops earring and a pair of white sneakers. She wants to show her actual personality in first impression because she believes that fake things don't last long. She don't want to give him any wrong indication of being sweet, innocent etc. By nature she is very loyal so she doesn't want to fake anything because no one could behave fake for their whole life. Sunaina wants to check Abhay's patience, so she reached café half an hour late. When she has reached cafe, Abhay is already present there waiting for her eagerly. He dressed up in all black branded tee-shirt, denim and sneakers. He was sitting impatiently for her and when meet her, immediately start questioning her that why she gets late on her first meeting. He told her that she had wasted his half an hour. He told in high tone that he don't like unpunctual people. Sunaina smiles and said "*yes I know but don't you think of asking reason why I was late and where I was stuck in before shouting like this*". Abhay understood immediately and changed the topic. He asked her what she want to have in food. Sunaina replied, anything you order. Abhay asked for menu to the waiter and ordered food as per his choice. He didn't bother to ask her again what she want. After ordering, Abhay asked her to tell about herself. And also what she is doing and what are her future plans. Sunaina replied that she is also doing engineering from the same institute where he is doing his engineering. Sunaina told him that she never saw him in college. Abhay replied that he had attended very few classes and his attendance were managed by his known in management team. And most of the time he was busy in his business or chilling at room. He also told her that he can't bear hot summer and especially south summer with lots of humidity. Sunaina replied "*For achieving goal in life, we should have to work hard whether it's hot or cold, no matter what.*" She also told him her opinion that if they will work hard now then only they have a bright future. On this context, Abhay laughed and replied "*No one's future becomes brighter with hard work, one should have to do smart work instead.*" Sunaina asked him then what she should do? Abhay smiled and replied her that if she will marry him then her future will be automatically brighter and successful. While saying all these his face was full of arrogance and attitude. His eyebrows were lifted and a side devil smile on his face. Sunaina was observing all his expressions, body language and his words usage.

They had conversation for almost two hours and Sunaina was not very happy with his behavior and thought process. While finishing their food and coffee Sunaina replied that her career is on priority for her and she wants to achieve success by her ability and not by marrying someone rich. She also told him that she wants to be financially independent and that also by self-hard work and not by anyone's help.

Abhay and Sunaina had a long discussion on this. Abhay is showing her that he is rich and have his own business and if a girl marry him then she doesn't need to work outside. She can join his company directly at senior position. He had also told her that his parents are renowned persons in the city but they were staying separately due to their work profile. His mother was a social worker and she didn't have time for family and neither his father spends time at home. He smiles and says in a funny way that his mother did well-fare for the society other than her family and so he doesn't want working wife like his mom.

Sunaina understands his emotions and asked him to try to understand his mother. A mother always loves her children no matter what. May be she has some reasons for all this she was doing. Abhay immediately changed the topic by saying that lets have some coffee. He doesn't want to talk much about his family in first introduction. Sunaina told him that she is getting late and she have to reach hostel before its closing time. By saying these she left. Abhay doesn't force her to stay. He asked her, "*Shall I drop you?*" Sunaina refused and replied that she can go by her own. Abhay doesn't forced her again. After meeting her, Abhay went to his friend's room to chill. And after meeting him Sunaina gets more confused because of her bad experiences and she doesn't want to fall in any trap again. There is a difference in her feelings for him before and after meeting him. Now she felt sympathy for him because despite of he belongs to a rich family but he had a disturbed childhood and lacking in family attention. They have uncountable money but family members are not living together to enjoy it and on the other side Sunaina belongs to a very close family where each and everything was celebrated together. And she had already faced heart break with such kind of guy from disturbed family. So she wants to control her sympathy feeling for him and not want to repeat her history again. She discussed all this with her roommate Ruhani. But Ruhani told her that she is over-thinking and she should give another chance to Abhay. All guys are not the same and all families are also not same. He is a rich guy and most of the rich guys are little arrogant and which is normal. She also recalls her past conversation again that if she will marry him than her future will be secured and can fulfill her dream easily. Marrying him is like a love cum arrange marriage and her parents are also happier in this marriage. Both side parents were already agreed to this marriage and as they both are in same college so they can go for date also like other unmarried couples which will fulfill her teenage dream of doing a love marriage.

Ruhani tried to do her complete brainwash and she gets succeeded also. At some point Sunaina also started dreaming of doing a love marriage with Abhay. She thought that if she will do love marriage to a random guy may be her parents will not agree for some reason and if she agreed to marry Abhay, everyone will be happily agreed for their marriage and she doesn't have to do much effort to convince them as the proposal is from their side. And if parents will get involved then there will be zero chances of getting cheated again. She has started thinking of all these possible aspects of marrying Abhay. She has also consoled herself that may be after some more meetings with him, she might understand him better.

Next day Abhay called her and asked her for movie. She is not comfortable going alone, so she asked him for taking one of her friend along with her. Abhay agreed and says, don't worry my friends are also going. After hearing this, Sunaina asked her friend Ruhani and Divya for movie. She again gets late for the movie as she returned late from college. They also get late due to some issue with local trains. They reached half an hour late from the movie time and movie has already started. Abhay was angry because of her late coming habit and didn't talk to her during that whole evening. He did not sit with her to punish her and teach her lesson for late coming. But this new version of Sunaina is effect less and she observed all his behavior but didn't show any reaction on her face. Rather she enjoyed watching movie sitting near Divya, eating popcorn and sandwich they bought. She talked to rest of the guys and her friend Ruhani and Divya. She behaved like nothing happened and not bothering anything at all.

Ruhani understood the things happening around her and she asked Sunaina whether she fought with Abhay. Sunaina denies and told her nothing happened between them. Abhay took Ruhani's contact no and called her to ask about Sunaina that why she is so rude and damn care. Ruhani told him all her past experiences. Two days passed without any calls. After two days, Abhay called Sunaina again and asked her whether she is angry or what? Sunaina replied that she is not angry but busy in her college assignments. Abhay without asking her further questions and to change the topic asked her for going out to some mall for shopping as he told he is not very good in shopping and he has to buy a sari for his mother. He told that he doesn't understand the quality of cloths and latest female fashion. He told her that being a girl she can do it better. So he requested her to go with him. Sunaina agreed to go with him.

Sunaina wore a casual attire and reached the mall on time. Abhay reached late today so she have to wait for twenty minutes alone but she passed her time by calling her mom. When she have seen Abhay coming towards her, she drop the call and welcome him and greeting him by saying hello and asked him *"Hows your day?"* Abhay simply smiles and says it's good but now after seeing you it will be wonderful (speaks in a flirty way). Sunaina smiles and moved on towards the sari outlet on the ground floor. She asked the shopkeeper bhaiya to show latest trendy, south silk saris and started seeing one by one and also bargaining with shopkeeper bhaiya. While Abhay asked her to take one sari for herself, Sunaina refused to take sari as they are very expensive and she don't want to take any such expensive gifts from him. But Abhay insists her to select something for herself. After so much of pressurizing, Sunaina agrees to take something small or less expensive. She has taken some random, less expensive hair accessories for herself and a south silk saree for his mom. Abhay paid the bill and while paying, told Sunaina that she has a middle class mentality because she didn't buy anything for herself. Sunaina replied, when she will start earning then she will buy expensive stuffs for herself with her self-earned money. Abhay replied, all this are middles class excuses of not buying expensive things. He again told her that if she will marry him, she don't have to think for money like this. He told that he have money and she will buy only expensive, branded things. He also told her that his ex-girlfriend never thinks twice before shopping branded, expensive things, whether she is paying it or not. She always slayed and had classy look. She had never been for street shopping but always shop from international brands. She was a spoil child of rich dad. Sunana replied, "*Just like you, you both are made for each other. Why don't you marry that girl?*" Abhay replied that his mom doesn't like her because she likes mature girl for me otherwise I will suffer in life. Sunaina asked him, "*Do you also believe the same?*" Abhay replied that his believe doesn't matter and if he will not listen to them then he have to loose all his property and business.

Sunaina again interrupted, "*Do you have your own mind? God has given us power to think what is better and what is not. It doesn't mean that your mom is incorrect but do you also agree with her or simply doing without knowing what you want.*" Sunaina speaks in louder voice and a bit irritated by his immature behavior.

Abhay has started requesting her, "*Please stop, why are you behaving like my parents. We are on a date and you are spoiling it.*" Sunaina has again started screaming, "*A Date? Who told you that we are on a date? I simply come to meet you because you need help for selecting sari for your mother. And for your kind information that we are not on any date. As now all shopping is done, I am leaving now."*

Now Abhay really gets scared of her strange behavior. He has started walking behind her without saying anything. After getting out of the mall, Abhay asked her, "*Shall I drop you to your hostel?*" Sunaina replied yes and get into his car. The whole way to the hostel, both were silent in the car. He dropped her in front of her hostel gate and left without saying anything.

Till two weeks they didn't call each other. While Sunaina is being feeling guilty for her misbehavior with Abhay, so she asked Ruhani for advice. Ruhani told her to say sorry to him and call him. Sunaina partially agreed and called him but decided not to apologize.

Sunaina called Abhay and speak politely as nothing happened. She asked him for going out as she want to talk to him. She also asked him to come to her hostel for pick up. Abhay replied her that if she wants to talk to him then she should come and he will not go for any pick up service. Sunaina has been requesting him again that it's month end now and she have one week left to get her expenses from her parents, so she is asking him to pick up her. Abhay in a voice of revenge replied "*That day you gave me so much lecture on not taking help and not using anyone's money, today you are asking help and money from me.*"

Sunaina replied, "*I am not asking money, I am just borrowing from you because I don't have money right now but when I will get my pocket money I will refill petrol in your car. Today I don't have money to come to meet you.*" Abhay replied in a strong voice, "*it's none of my business.*" Sunaina gets irritated by his arrogant behavior and replied him that she has changed her mind and she will not meet him till she have started earning money. By saying this last words she hung up the call.

For almost 2 months, they didn't call each other. One day all of sudden, Abhay called Sunaina at 8:00 in the evening while she is in her hostel room with Ruhani and they both were watching movies in laptop. Sunaina picked up his call. Abhay in a calm and pampering tone requested her to come out of her hostel as he wants to meet her. He is being waiting outside her hostel. Sunaina forbid him which is reasonable. She told him that it's not the time to meet any outsider and so I will not come out. Abhay was drunk that day and in drunk condition, he has been screaming loudly in front of her hostel that if she will not come out of her hostel to meet him then he will not leave.

Sunaina gets angered by his arrogant behavior. So she had threatened him in phone that if he will scream loud again then she will be bound to call police to arrest him. In the mean-time Ruhani from background told Abhay in call that Sunaina will meet him tomorrow and for god sake leave now. Abhay told Ruhani that he wants to hear it from Sunaina. While Sunaina has refused to say yes. To control the situation, Ruhani promised him on behalf of Sunaina that she will bring her to meet him tomorrow. On saying this, Sunaina gets angered upon Ruhani and argued with her that does she on her side or his side? Ruhani replied that she want to see both of them happy together. Ruhani tried her level best to convince her to meet him next day. Finally Sunaina agreed to meet him but she doesn't want to go alone. She agreed on one condition that if Ruhani will go along with her then only she will meet him the next day. She told her that if she will also meet him then only she can understand how arrogant he is.

Next day after college, Ruhani, Abhay, Sunaina and Ajay (Abhay's friend) meet in a nearby café. Abhay clarify them that he was angry that day so he speaks like that but after that he regrets. He wants to do friendship again with Sunaina. Sunaina has also started complaining in front of everyone *"That day he insulted me in front of all so if he really felt regret for that than he should say sorry to me in front of all."* Abhay agreed with Sunaina's condition and invited all his friends in a party including Ruhani. Party scheduled on Sunday and Abhay named it as Patch-Up party. Sunaina has also get excited because she wants to observe him on that party as she had realized that might be she became judgmental about him without knowing him completely.

Sunaina wore her favorite traditional Indigo salwar suit which her parents told her to wear on their first meeting. She is very happy on that day as she feels like she has won the battle between them and he had realized his fault. While the truth is something else as Abhay is also self –centered and can't handle rejection. So he did all such drama of feeling guilty so that he could get her back in his life.

Sunaina and Ruhani had reached the party venue on time. It's again a lavish party with all rich friends of Abhay. While Sunaina was thinking how Abhay will say sorry to her in front of so many people. In the meantime, Abhay took the mike and a bouquet and announced to all that he loves Sunaina a lot and can't live his life without her. And now its Sunaina's turn to accept his proposal.

Everyone in that hall are eagerly waiting for her reply. Sunaina gets both shocked and annoyed by his announcement as she was not ready for this.

Everyone present at that party along with her friend Ruhani has been started cheering up for her loudly by calling her name Sunainaaaa…aa..Sunainaaa. When all these are happening, Sunaina comes under peer pressure and everyone present in that party has been requesting her to accept him. They all are telling her, *"common Sunaina, say YES. We all are waiting for hearing yes from you. He loves you a lot and no one else will love you like him. He is most eligible bachelor in our college. Say him yes".*

Sunaina in a very low voice *"Give me some time to think".* But under so much of pressure at last she said yes to him without further thinking. After hearing yes from her, all has started screaming by their name and music has also started in the background. All have started dancing, screaming and hugging each other like India won world cup. All of sudden, Sunaina and Abhay's eyes get connected and both smiled and blushed together. These party has been turned into a happy moment for both of them.

While returning back to hostel, Sunaina has been rethinking about what happened in that party and asked Ruhani with a doubt *"Is this all planned? Am I did correct by saying him yes?"* Ruhani replied her with confidence that she did great. She also told her that all rich guys are somehow arrogant and haughty but she have the caliber to change him. Ruhani also told her *"See he had thrown such a huge party only for you which shows he loves you a lot. You are overthinking. He is a nice guy with a great heart, just a girl like you is missing in his life. If I would be in your place and he proposes me then I would immediately say him yes."* Sunaina laughs and replied, *"Shall I tell him about your feelings for him."* Ruhani warned her, *"Don't do such foolish things. Please try to understand that he loves only you. Your future will be better with him and you are not at all serious."* Sunaina replied, that she will make her future by her own and she don't need anyone's help. She also told her that she will do job no matter her husband will be rich or poor or have a large bank balance. She loves her independence and she won't sacrifice it for anyone.

Ruhani told her that she doesn't have to sacrifice her independence with him, he is a nice guy and he will give her complete independence. He deserves a girl like her and they look good together. To lighter the conversation Ruhani told Sunaina that one day when her friend Sunaina will become rich then she will forget her poor friends like Ruhani. Sunaina laughed a lot on this and has started her leg pulling. Sunaina asked Ruhani to marry Abhay so that she will become rich and she could also showed tantrums like a rich spoil girl as he like spoiled girls. Both of them get asleep after all this girls talk.

Next day when Sunaina and Ruhani are in college, Abhay also came to college at afternoon in hot summer. He had never used to eat food in college canteen but to spend time with her, he has started eating canteen food. Sunaina has been observing all these without telling him anything. She has been liking the changes in him. Now he is not showing off his money power and rich man tantrums. It seems he has realized that others also have self-respect. Now Sunaina also starts believing that his changes in behavior is because of her and in future she could change him into a humble and modest person. But she wants to take time to trust him completely due to her past worst experiences. As she have so much of bad chapters in her life that she don't want another one and also not to get hurt again.

When Sunaina's parents has asked her about Abhay Malhotra, she told them that she needs some time to decide and understand him.

While she was admiring him for his change in behavior and is building trust on him. He have done something weird again which irritates her and crashed her trust on him. And she again come to the same point whether to continue with him or not. Although here everything is perfect whether his effort for good behavioral change or her career security and financial stability. Possibility of love marriage, family's happiness everything is here in their relationship but then also something is missing and she is unable to feel the love and respect for him as one should feel when fell in love. She is still confused for him. To understand him better and find the missing loop before taking any decision Sunaina wants to meet him again and so she has planned a movie date with him. Sunaina asked Ruhani also for the movie. Sunaina has still remembered his behavior during last movie so she and Ruhani reached movie hall on time. As Sunaina was recalling all these, suddenly Abhay arrived and asked her permission to sit nearby in the movie hall. She agreed and nodded head. She is watching movie and observing his activities without telling him anything.

During the interval, Abhay and his friend has gone to get some popcorns for all. And by chance Abhay has forgotten his mobile on the seat. Sunaina is sitting on next to his seat and his phone starts ringing. Sunaina have seen that one of his ex-girlfriend is calling him and after two miscalls she has stopped calling. In the meantime when Abhay was searching his mobile for doing payment, he realized that he has forgotten his mobile on the seat. Immediately he asked his friend to pay the bill and run for his phone. When Abhay have seen the miss-calls then he gets little nervous and asked Sunaina, *"Did you pick up any call on my phone?"* Sunaina replied, *"No I have n't received but your ex-girlfriend is calling you two times."* Abhay gets tensed and replied, *"Yes sometimes she called me when she need any help but we are moved on and you don't worry for this"*. Sunaina replied, "*I am not worrying for anything else than this movie's climax. I came here to watch movie only and not to listen your unnecessary explanations*." Abhay gets surprised by her reply and asked her that generally girls bother if their boyfriend's get call from their ex-girlfriend. Sunaina replied "*I am not like other stupid girls. I don't mind who is calling you or not*." Abhay replied, "*You are an ideal girlfriend and I am lucky to have you in my life as partner and will be happiest when we will get married."* Sunaina told him to shut his mouth and let her watch the movie as she don't want to miss the climax. Abhay felt little weird by her behavior that why she is not bothering or feeling jealousy at all.

Love Note: Money helps you in buying gifts for your love but can't buy someone's love for you. Love needs care, pamper, loyalty, forgiveness, trust and respect for each other. Money can't buy it. Girls' sixth sense can sense it whether one's love is genuine or not. If someone loves you because you are rich then he /she can easily move to someone who is richer than you. Respect and Trust is two important things in love without which money can't help.

Love at First Sight

Exams are around the corner and all the final year students are busy in exam's preparation. This is the last semester exam to become an Engineer. During final semester, most of the Engineering Students gets busy in final year projects and getting prepared for campus interviews because of which bunking classes is common. Sunaina and Ruhani are also doing the same. Their daily routine is to attend two to three classes and then getting back to final year project preparation. Usually they came back to their room by 3:00pm and had their meal and power nap for one hour and then did their assignments with evening hot cup of filter coffee at 4:30pm and study for exams till 2:00am.

One day morning Ruhani got a call from her home that her mother is not well and she have to go to her hometown. Ruhani called Sunaina to see off her. While Sunaina and Ruhani are waiting for the cab near a petrol pump at little distance from their hostel then they have noticed a stranger guy is staring them constantly and talking with someone in bluetooth. Sunaina and Ruhani thought that may be this guy hasn't realized that he is staring them because he was in call. When Ruhani's cab arrived and she left then Sunaina have doubt on that stranger guy because he had finished his petrol refilling but still standing there and staring at her. Sunaina got scared of his behavior so she has started walking faster towards her hostel. She also called Ruhani for feeling safe and asked her to talk to her till she reach the hostel. Sunaina has taken short route to mislead that stranger guy because he was following her. After reaching hostel, Sunaina thought that she had deceived that biker boy but after a while she saw from her balcony that he had found her hostel address and was standing right in front of the gate and was doing some arm motions showing victory. By seeing these Sunaina gets confirmed that he was intentionally following her.

Next day when Sunaina is returning back from her college to her hostel then she noticed that biker boy who was following her yesterday. She had recognized him even with helmet but today she is not scared of him because she was surrounded with a crowd of students on the road. She thought that if she realize any danger then she will immediately shout for help as she knew that if she will shout then the boys (mostly students) present there will come to save her and might be beat him.

To watch his activities and to see his face Sunaina moved to a mobile recharge shop. She saw that stranger guy is roaming there with his bike and helmet on. When she came out of the shop again that biker boy has started following her. Sunaina walked faster than her usual pace and took a deep breath after reaching her room. These kind of incident never happened in her life and she never thought that someone will follow her like crazy one and at the same time she is also scared. She thought that why this stranger person is following her and what would be his intentions. She is curious to see his face without helmet and want to ask him for what he is following her.

After two days, she has to go to college for admit card. So she wish to see that stranger guy again nearby college so that she can solve the mystery and also scold him for following her. She thought of asking him does he know her or anything he wants to say.

Next day after collecting the admit card, Sunaina has gone to the juice corner nearby her college so that she can see that biker boy again. As her intuition says, that biker boy will come again and she could see his face. She ordered juice simply to pass time. She took the juice and sit there so that she can wait for some time until the biker boy arrived. After few minutes that biker boy has appeared for real and without his helmet. He is driving his bike to and fro in front of that juice corner to see her. And Sunaina is observing him, she saw a tall handsome guy, rigid physique, tanned skin with sharp face features is riding a bike. And his silky flowing hair has stolen her heart. He is slanting his bike while driving and moving to and fro. Sunaina's eyes get stuck on him unknowingly. She felt cool breeze in hot Chennai summer and gets attracted by him, his flying hair, his bike stunts although she knows all these are stupidity.

After a while Sunaina came out of the juice corner with smile on her face and walking towards her hostel. She is laughing at herself and wanted that stranger guy to follow her again. After few minutes, she saw that biker boy again. He is passing in front of her and drive up to some distance and return back and cross her again. He did this four to five times to get her attention. Sunaina is pretending as if she haven't noticed him. After he left Sunaina is still searching him on road and wants him to follow her again. She knew that all these are stupidity but she is enjoying it. She felt surprised by her own behavior and laughed at herself. She feels happy to see him whom she was scared of few days back.

Her final semester exams after a week and to avoid distractions, she has stopped going outside for that complete week.

One week later, when she is returning back from college, she have seen that biker boy again flaunting his silky hair flowing in the air. On that day, she have looked at his eyes for the first time and felt attraction at first sight. While looking at each other's eyes crossing each other in front of the college, they fell in love without knowing each other's name, caste, past and future. After that day Sunaina had seen him many times till her last exam day. After that only project submission and campus interviews are remaining and then she have to return back to her hometown.

Sunaina and Ruhani always been to a renowned temple nearby their hostel every week on Thursdays mainly for their *prasadam* which tastes like home food. Sunaina's last exam finished on Thursday so she asked Ruhani to come along with her to the temple. Ruhani was not feeling well on that day so Sunaina have to go alone to that temple. While going to temple alone suddenly she got a call from Abhay which makes her upset. She have lost her faith on him so she doesn't want to talk to him. As her exams are over and she knows that she have few days left to go back to her hometown, so she desperately want to escape from all this love chaos and worst chapters. When going to the worship place she is murmuring to herself and requesting god *"Oh god! Please remove all these unnecessary love chaos and vanish all these unwanted persons from my life and send one to my life who would be my future husband."* Before reaching temple, she is praying to god saying that she is fed up of all these stupid guys and their fake love. So remove them all and send only her future husband to her life. Just after praying she saw a light flashed behind her and when she turned back, she saw a bike at some distance whose head light is flashing bright. She has tried to confirm whether this biker is the same biker boy or not but she couldn't see his face due to strong beam of light on her face. Sunaina reached the temple and entered inside. She does her evening prayer and then have *prasadam*. After one hour, she came out and while walking towards her hostel she have seen that bike again and when she came closer to that bike then she recognized the bike and the biker. She gets shocked because it was the same biker boy standing there. And at the same time she gets angered to God because she had just prayed to god that next whoever person she will meet would be her partner only and god send him. She thought that god has not taken her prayer seriously and was in mood of playing more games with her emotions. She is talking to god in aggressive way *"How do you think this biker boy could be my husband, why are you still playing with my emotions."*

On the other side that biker boy is following her. When she walk that bike also move and when she stops then that bike also stops. After some time that biker boy slowly came near to her and ask her *"What's the time?"* Sunaina was already upset and not in a mood to talk to anyone. That biker boy again asked her *"Mam can you tell me time, you are wearing a watch?"* She has abruptly stopped walking and asked him boldly, *"Are you following me?"* That biker gets shocked by her reply and with a trembling voice replied her, *"n..no…nooo …n…nooo I am not following you, my home on the way."* Sunaina gets irritated by his behavior and asked him rudely again "*why are you lying? Where is your home?*" He replied, "*Nearby your hostel.*" Sunaina asked him again, "*Where is your original home?"* He replied, "*I have home in many places like Delhi, Chennai and Mumbai*"….Sunaina laughs on his reply and thinking that she is talking to a real bluff master. She says in sarcastic way, "Again I found a liar, all thanks to god".

Biker boy told her *"I know your name Sunaina from the very first day of you entered the college. I heard while some students are shouting your name and teasing you. Then I searched you in social media but couldn't find. I had sent friendship request to all whose name is Sunaina and in return they all blocked me and my social media handle also gets blocked. Now as I told you everything will you give me your Social media handle?*" Sunaina replied boldly, *"I don't talk to strangers then how could I give you my social media Id."* After listening this from her, the biker boy has started his bike and moved forward. Sunaina gets astonished by his behavior and thought that what type of boy is this? She thought that he will request her one more time.

While she was thinking all these, she saw at some distance that biker boy had stopped his bike again and waiting for her to come. When Sunaina reached nearby him, before his saying anything, she starts speaking and asking him to share his social media Id and if she liked it then she will contact him back via text. He trembled and smiled on her behavior and shared his Id instantly. She wants to check out his social media profile so send him friendship request and ordered him to accept it immediately. Then she asked him what he is doing – studying or job? He replied that he is studying in 3rd year Mechanical branch in same college. She thought that he is lying again because she have never seen him in college. Biker boy told her that he has been seeing her from the first day of her college. In actual he was that sweet and simple guy who had stopped other students from teasing her on her first day. Then slowly he asked her mobile number. She smiled at his confidence but denied to give him number. She told him that she will not give her number to any stranger. She noticed that his hands are shivering while holding phone so she asked his number instead of giving own number. He instantly gave his number and tell his name, Kabir in a trembling voice. Sunaina is smiling at his behavior but didn't showed him. After getting his number, she said good bye to him and entered the hostel. Kabir is feeling out of the world as he got chance to talk to her after three and half years of long waiting. It seems like an achievement for him.

From next day, she have not seen him for two weeks and gets worried for him and searching him while walking on road nearby college. She has searched his social media profile but not found any update about his current location. Once she thinks of calling him but again she don't want to seem desperate in front of him. So she didn't call him but eagerly waiting for him and regularly going to College Street, juice corner and that mobile recharge shop without any necessary work. If she didn't have any work in these places then she does her roommates work like mobile recharge, print outs, shopping grocery etc., and having juice every day from that particular juice shop.

One day evening while she is returning back from that juice shop, she noticed a local boy carrying a huge gift bag in his hand standing nearby her hostel gate. When she reached nearby him, he has given that gift parcel to her and ran away. At the moment when she is holding the gift, she thought that the biker boy is back and he has sent this gift to her. She have searched his name on that gift but it has no name written on it. She brought it up stair to her room and showed her friends already sitting in her room. She told them that she got this parcel at down stair and an unknown small boy has given her this and ran away. Her friends gets excited to open the gift and also teasing her that she have a secret admirer. She is thinking that might be Kabir wants to surprise her. Three of them has opened the gift bag. In that huge bag, they found 10 gifts wrapped with colorful gift papers and small poetry notes along each gifts. Ruhani and Divya were excited to open these gifts and to read the poetries. It has a pair of branded denim trouser and a tee-shirt, chocolates, flowers, a huge cards and a bottle of red wine. This gift bag also includes vibhuti and a pen with best wishes written on it for her future exams. Sunaina is feeling special while opening these gifts. Sunaina felt happier because she thought that Kabir has gifted her all this to surprise her before exams. She had shared chocolates and red wine with her hostel friends Ruhani and Divya and also flaunting them about her secret admirer, Kabir.

After a month she have seen Kabir once again in front of college roaming on his bike , to and fro, and his silky straight hairs becomes more silky and are flying in the air and synchronized with his bike movement. Like earlier he is riding his bike and bending extreme left and right. Sunaina gets speechless after seeing him with a big winning smile on his face. He is wearing a blue denim, a printed tee-shirt and converse shoes and driving his red bike. Without caring about other students and surroundings, she is constantly looking at his eyes and smiling unknowingly. Kabir understood that she has been started liking him. Sunaina came out of that juice corner and had started walking towards the hostel and after sometime looking behind to confirm whether Kabir is following her or not. Kabir understood her wish and has started following her like before. This time Sunaina is not scared or worried rather she is happy that he is following her. When she is about to reach her hostel, she has stopped walking and turned like before to ask him, "*Are you following me?*" Kabir without understanding her tricky question, simply replied, "*No my home is on the way.*" Sunaina smiled on his simplicity and asked him "*Where was you these days?*" He replied that he went to his hometown. Sunaina starts making fun of him that he lied about his original home on their first meeting. Kabir replied seriously, "*I never lied. Here I have been staying with my Aunty which I consider as my home and I have been to my hometown where my mother live. And wherever I stayed in past, all were my home. So I told that I have home at many places.*" Sunaina laughed at his words and still thinking what type of confident liar he is. While she was laughing at him, Kabir thought that this is the right time to ask her for a coffee date. So Kabir asked Sunaina, "*Will you go for coffee with me?*" Sunaina laughed at him and replied that she will not go anywhere with a stranger. Then Kabir asked her that if she is not comfortable to go with him then no issue, let's have coffee here on road. He asked her to bring cups and hot milk from the hostel and he will bring coffee sachet from the shop. Sunaina had prepared answers in her mind before telling him that she never goes with stranger but the reply from him is un expected. She gets shocked by his reply and her serious face turns into laughter.

After non-stop laughing, she again pretends like a strict person. After his prompt and weird reply, she got impressed by him and thought that maybe he help her in finding a laptop repairing shop. So she asked him that does he knows any laptop repairing shop as her laptop is not working and she don't know any repairing shop in Chennai.

Kabir is very much prompt in all such things. He thought this is the chance to impress her so he took it very seriously. Without losing a minute, he called two to three repairing shops, noted their address and spoke in their local language which is another plus point for him to impress her.

After noticing his prompt reply and immediate action, Sunaina agreed to go with him next day and she clarified him not to think it as date. Kabir smiled at her words and nodded head to her orders. He asked her that he will come to pick up her at 10:00am but Sunaina refused his pick up proposal and told him that she will come to the main road away from her hostel and from there she will go with him. Kabir agreed to all her conditions whatever she is saying to him.

Next day, Sunaina woke up early and get ready. She wore her favorite clothes. Same day Kabir had cleaned up both his bike and his hair for that extra shine and impression. He reached to the location before time and as usual Sunaina reached fifteen minutes after time. While going she was thinking that Kabir will also shout at her like Abhay did for late coming. But when she reached there, she got surprised by seeing his smiling face and happy greetings. He has not asked her anything regarding late coming. Rather he is telling her that if she had allowed him to pick up her then it would be easy for her to reach here. Then he asked Sunaina to sit on back seat of his bike. Sunaina felt awkward to sit on his bike and told him that she will go by her own and meet him directly at the repairing shop. Kabir understood immediately and take out his backpack and slide it on his back to create a distance between them while sitting on bike. Sunaina smiled at his gesture and told him that now she is comfortable to sit on his bike.

Kabir keeps on telling jokes while driving bike so that Sunaina will not get bored. To make her laugh he even ready to make fun of himself. He is a true entertainer and Sunaina actually didn't get bored for a minute while travelling with him for two hours to reach that shop. Sunaina finds him witty and an awesome companion. Finally they reached the shop and handover her laptop to the repairing person. That repairing person told them that he needs 4 to 5 hours for repairing. On hearing this, Kabir gets happier as he got another chance to ask her again for coffee. Out of excitement, he told the repairing person to take six hours and complete his work properly. Then he asked Sunaina for coffee in a nearby coffee café day in mall. And he told her that after coffee they will do shopping also in that mall. He told her that it's too hot outside and waiting in repairing shop is waste of time. Cafes and malls are fully air-conditioned so it will be comfortable to hang out inside mall, he said. Sunaina kept on smiling on his explanations to convince her. At last she said him lets have coffee together and then shopping. Kabir get excited on hearing this as all these are happening whatever he had wished before.

Kabir has told her about his family and about himself without any filter. She told him that he is junior to her and if she wishes she could ragged him in college. He told her that next year he will also pass out college then who will recognize who is junior and senior. She asked him that how he has managed his studies and attendance without going to the college.

"I have settings for attendance and have 36 back papers which will be cleared someday", he said. For Sunaina, having 36 back papers and such chill behavior is not normal. She told him that he is a day dreamer and without doing any effort how come he can clear his papers. He tried all possible ways to impress her but his attitude towards studies makes her upset. She thought that this is another sample of over confidence. But she likes his wittiness and prompt replies. She also thought that this boy needs proper guidance and rest all are good in him. She likes his behavior towards her. She also noticed him behaving well with other economically weaker people like waiter, guard and beggar and specially moved by his respect for women. She also gets impressed by him that he understands her mind without telling him anything and he behaved indifferent with rich and poor.

Kabir has also told her about his ex-girlfriend who had left him and told him that she would meet him only when he would completed his B.tech engineering. That girl was not loving you and she was an opportunist, forget her, Sunaina said. He asked Sunaina her choices of food and told her that he likes Chennai Biryani, the most. He is doing fun all the time and continuously trying to makes her laugh. While laughing on his jokes, her eyes get filled with tears because she is recalling her horrible past and comparing them with his behavior. She is thinking that how he has no regrets for anything happened in his past and neither worried for his future. He is a real free soul which is free from all social boundaries. Sunaina had never met any person like him. She understood that he is trying to impress her but his style of impressing is different from others. He makes her comfortable up to the extent that she forgets he is a stranger whom she knows from the current day only. She don't know what is in her destiny but she will remember this day and him forever, she thinks.

When Kabir saw her teary eyes, he has started teasing her by calling her "*yaadon ki baraat*" means past memory lane. Sunaina gets astonished that he is making fun of her instead of asking anything about her past. While Kabir is smart enough and understood the pain behind her tears so he is teasing her to lighten up her sad mood. And these actually works, she immediately burst into laughter.

"You are roaming with me then what about your girlfriend if she knows." she asked him in a tricky way. *"I already told you that I don't have any girlfriend"*, he replied. *"How is this possible that you don't have any girlfriend? You are young, handsome and you have bike also then how are you still single?"* she asked with curiosity. Kabir replied with smile, *"Once upon a time I had one but she also left me for no reason. She belongs to here and was studying in my class. After one year, she left me and I took admission in engineering. And she went somewhere else and started avoiding me and also was not receiving my phone calls. After few days I get to know that she was in love with someone else."*

Sunaina has been co-relating her past with his past and laughs loudly and tell him that her girlfriend had made him fool for one year. How she could left you if she truly loved you, she said. Kabir smiled and said, *"I knew that and I cried a lot for her but after that I moved on in my life"*. *"If I was in your life instead of that stupid girl, I had never let you cry. I had been taken care of your happy soul and kept it happy for sure", she murmured.* After six hours of long conversation, coffee and then lunch, they have been to pick up the laptop but that repairing person told them that it has some hardware issues so he couldn't return it today. He asked them to take it next day. Sunaina got angry and started arguing with that repairing person that why he had not informed them earlier. After wasting six hours he is telling these, she said. She had saved money from her expenses for this speaker repairing and now he is asking to pay for hardware. She has decided that she will not going to pay any extra penny for this new issue in laptop. She told him that it's his fault so he has to repair hard disc by his own and she will pay only for the speaker which was decided earlier and she came for.

Kabir also shows anger to the repairing person but happy from inside because he got another chance to meet her. After arguing with the laptop repairer, they came out of the shop and get on the bike for going back to hostel. On the way, Sunaina has shared her mobile number as now she trust him completely. After getting her number, Kabir asked her that what if her boyfriend see them on his bike while dropping her to the hostel. She doesn't want to tell him about Abhay so she replied that she don't have any boyfriend. She lied as she don't want to loose Kabir's friendship and his attention.

While driving Kabir told her that he have exam next day morning and so he is driving faster to reach home early and can study a bit before exam. She gets surprised by his damn care attitude and asked him why he hadn't tell these earlier. Laptop could be repaired some other day then why you have wasted whole day with me, she asked. "*Are you ragging me?*" he asked. She told him that being a senior, she can rag him anytime and he have to show respect to her. Kabir replied, "Y*ou already did ragging and I always have respect for you*." Sunaina laughs louder.

Kabir has dropped her near the hostel gate and has given her a packet full of chocolates and a meal packed for her dinner. He thought if they will be late then she wouldn't get her dinner at hostel so he packed food for her. Sunaina's eyes get filled with tears again by seeing his caring nature like her mother. Kabir smiled and teased her again "*Ooh meri yaadon ki baaraat*" means again you been to the past memory lane. He is instantly changing the sad moment into happier by his prompt replies.

That night Sunaina couldn't sleep and is sitting on terrace all alone till 3:00am. She is questioning to god that why god has done this to her? Few days back she had accepted Abhay's proposal and now Kabir came in her life. She is questioning to god that why Kabir came into her life if Abhay is there. And if Kabir is in her future then why she had accepted Abhay. She also thought that there is no future with Kabir then why she saw him outside the temple on that day after praying god for life-partner only.

She is also worried about the lie she told to Kabir. She felt guilty for hiding her relationship status because if Kabir got serious about their relationship, then she can't accept him neither reject him. She liked him but she knew that there is no future between them because her parents will never accept him and she can't go against them. She gets puzzled between Kabir and Abhay because Abhay is her present boyfriend whom she already said yes and their parents are already involved in this relationship but she felt no love for him. On the contrary, Kabir is a stranger biker boy whom she knows from two days only and worried for him and lied to him as she is scared of loosing him but there is no future, she thought.

Next day at 6:00am, she has written a text message to Kabir that she had lied yesterday about her relationship status. She also wrote that she have a boyfriend who is also studied in their college. Kabir thought it in other ways, he thought that she must be testing him and indirectly proposing him as he had never seen her with anyone. So he laughs and told Sunaina that he knows.

Also she has informed him that she have to submit her project by next week, so till then she will not go anywhere. Then Kabir reminds her about her laptop left in the repairing shop. Sunaina has agreed to go for laptop pick up because she thought that she couldn't meet him anymore after her project submission as she has to return back to her native place. Kabir has asked her for a movie after laptop pick up. Sunaina also agreed for movie as this might be her last movie with him, she thought. They have decided to meet after his exam. She gets ready after his exam over but as usual reach the main road twenty minutes late. Kabir was waiting there and reached ten minutes before time. Sunaina said sorry to Kabir for the delay but Kabir smiles and appreciate her outfit and her appearance. Sunaina asked Kabir, *"I always came late but you never get angry on me why?"* Kabir replied, *"Best thing takes time to happen."* Sunaina gets blushed and to change the topic, asked him about his exams. Kabir replied, I had written exam for passing marks only. Sunaina gets surprised by his reply and asked him that why he is not taking his studies seriously. *"We all study for getting higher grades which is essential for our career growth and it will decide our future too. How are you so chill about your career and future?"* she asked. Kabir replied, *"I am chill because I am not a coward like others. I am ready to face my future."* Sunaina replied, *"Why are you not serious?"* Kabir replied, *"If I will be serious then I would be admitted in the hospital."*

Sunaina laughs and understood that he is a different type of person and she can't teach him anything so let him be like he is. She also thought that every person is different and if she is attracted by a person's nature then why she is trying to convert him like herself. She has promised to herself that she will never try to change him unless it's harmful. She liked his witty nature and doesn't want to change it for any reason as she met this kind of person for the first time in her life.

On the way Kabir has again asked her for confirmation about the text she had sent and her boyfriend. She said that she lied because she want to keep their friendship forever and she was confused about her boyfriend. Kabir asked her again, *"Why confused? Does he is not as good as me?"* Sunaina replied, "*No, you are the best and laughs louder*." She told him that after project submission she has to go back to her hometown which is very far away from Chennai and after that she could never meet him again. Kabir smiled and replied with positive attitude, *"Let's see madam and never say never and no one knows future so don't try to predict it."* Kabir has dropped her near hostel and again gave her packet full of chocolates, burger and juice for her dinner.

She was busy in her project preparation and presentation for the whole week. She wishes to meet Kabir again before leaving Chennai. So she called him and asked him for both movie and lunch. Kabir asked her, *"Will you go for coffee with me today?"* She understood his wish and agreed instantly. She told Kabir that she will go to campus interview next day and day after tomorrow, she would have to catch flight for her hometown.

Then Kabir told her that he will come to see off her. Sunaina don't want to meet him on last day because it will be tough for her to say good bye to him forever. While reaching to her hostel, she thanked Kabir for that surprise gift she received at hostel. Kabir replied that he has not sent any gift to her. Then who will be this secret admirer, she thought?

Her interview gone well and she got positive response from the interviewers but not received any offer letter yet. So she had not decided to come back to Chennai again. Next day, she missed the flight due to her unpunctuality. When she has informed her parents about this and other flight fares are too high and also unavailable for two days. Her parents immediately called Ruhani to help her, Ruhani called Abhay and asked him for help. She told him everything and request him to book confirm tickets for her either in train or in flight. Abhay did flight tickets for her and meet her to give the ticket. In the meantime, Kabir have seen them together and gets hurt. He thought that Sunaina had lied about her flight to avoid him and meeting her boyfriend. Sunaina has noticed him standing far away staring at her with upset face. She felt guilty for hurting him but later on she thought that it would be easier for him to forget her because they have no future. She has also decided not to call him to explain.

Next day she has arrived to the airport on time. She is happy because after long time she is going back to her home and meet her parents. She is also happy with memories of Kabir but sad because she is leaving him forever. Two hours journey has passed easily by seeing his photos in her phone and remembering his witty talks that he had told to her.

As she reached home, everyone came out to welcome her. Her siblings and cousins have planned outings with her. She is busy in all this family chaos for next two weeks.

Kabir also reached his hometown after his exams were finished.

One day, Sunaina is all alone at her home and all her family members has been gone to a family function. She has thought of calling Kabir. After thinking all aspects she has dialed his number. Kabir is driving his bike and his mom sitting on his backseat so her mom had picked up the call and said hello. Sunaina hung up the call as she thought that it may be a wrong number. After gathering courage, she called him again. Again his mother has picked up the call then Sunaina thought that may be Kabir is roaming with his girlfriend and has lied to her.

After dropping his mother in market almost half an hour later Kabir has called her back and said that he was with his mom and she had picked up the phone for two times as he was driving. He asked her that why she was disconnecting the call. She replied, *I thought that you were with your girlfriend and I don't want to disturb you both.*" Kabir laughed and replied that he don't have any girlfriend as he already told her. They have started talking every day to each other. Kabir told her everything he did the whole day. Sunaina told him partially as she don't want to get hurt like earlier. Life is a vicious cycle what you get from one, you are giving it to other. What Vinay does with her to be safe she is doing the same to Kabir.

Love Note: In current generation also Love at first Sight happens and people may fell in love without knowing anything about each other. But those who have not met anyone to fall in love, no need to worry because whoever is in your destiny, universe will send him/her to you at the right time. Surrender yourself to the destiny because what you know is already past and knowing future is not possible. So what we think good for us today may be not in future. And better option may be awaited in the future. Just believe in your destiny and leave rest all to it.

Physical Love vs Mental Love

Abhay's parents came to Sunaina's home to finalize their wedding date. Both families' want them get married soon and wish to see them together. Abhay's parent likes her a lot and they always wishes to have a daughter in law like her. Sunaina couldn't say in front of all that she don't want to marry Abhay Malhotra. She can't stay happy with him, she thinks. Although she knew very well that her parents will not accept Kabir as her groom but then also she wants to take a chance.

One day when Sunaina was sitting with her mother, she told her about Kabir. Sunaina's mother replied her that their marriage is not possible because no one in the family will agree for this marriage. Her mother was consoling her that Kabir belongs to different region and most important one year younger than her, not settled yet. He is still a student and not started earning yet while Abhay has secured future, she said. Sunaina is silently accepting all what her mother is telling to her and also believing that may be she is right. She had conveyed these to Kabir and told him that they should keep a distance in their relationship and shouldn't talk daily so that they will not get hurt later. But Kabir has complete faith on his love and he told her that he will convince everyone in her family. He is confident and positive about his belief that he could convince them all. Sunaina likes his positivity and confidence and have faith on him that he can manage everything.

The very next day, she got the job offer letter and as destiny had decided everything so she got another chance to move to Chennai and meet him. She has informed everyone that she got the job and have to leave for Chennai within 15 days. Family members are happy as she is going to do her first job but upset as well because she is there only for ten to fifteen days. Sunaina called Kabir to tell him the good news as she is excited for the job and meeting him again. Kabir gets excited by this news and committed her that he will be there forever for pick up and drop service from office to hostel and love to be her all time driver. She don't have to worry about travelling anywhere in Chennai, he said.

When Abhay heard about her job in Chennai then he also gets excited as he was there for his business and his back papers exam. Abhay called her to congratulate and asked her to give him company in flight as he is also going to Chennai on same day. Sunaina's parents forced her to go along with him as they thought that Sunaina and Abhay will get some more time to know each other. Lastly she agreed to go along with him in the same flight. For the very first time Sunaina has no complain with Abhay during the journey. She is happy during the journey as she is going to meet Kabir. While Abhay is thinking that Sunaina might be started liking him and forget all his faults.

After reaching Chennai, Kabir helped her a lot. From finding working hostel to all her necessities, everything is done by Kabir. He made a schedule so that he could attend his college as well as pick up and drop her to office and hostel. Firstly he dropped her to her office and then he goes to his college and in the evening after class finished, he picked up her from her office and then both of them go to coffee shop and after that drop her to the hostel. Kabir cares about her comfort and did all possible things to make her happy and not feeling lonely. He took her to new places in Chennai to make her familiar with the Chennai city. Sunaina had lived three and half years in Chennai but knew only few places and during her job of six months, she get to know as many places as some locals do. Every day after office they been to new places having Coffee date and explore new places, markets, movie halls, tourist spots. These became their daily routine and after all these he dropped her to hostel with food packets. In every weekends, they did their dinner together outside in some fancy restaurants.

One day Sunaina's father told her to meet Abhay and to discuss about their marriage locations, theme etc.. etc. Next day Sunaina met him as she can't say no to her father. But she had decided to tell him about her boyfriend Kabir and request him to reject the marriage proposal in front of both side parents. When she told Abhay that she had a boyfriend then he replied that he has no issue if she had any random boyfriend because his parents want them to get married and he also want to marry her. Sunaina gets upset by his reply as she knows that her family will never agree for Kabir and she have to marry Abhay without having any feelings for him. Next month is Abhay's birthday and he has invited Sunaina and Ruhani to his birthday party. After knowing about her boyfriend, he had assumed that he got permission to invite his ex-girlfriends in that party, so he had invited them too.

On his birthday party, he announced that he is going to marry Sunaina because his parents want her as their daughter in law and she is pretty enough to be someone's wife. After these announcement, Sunaina gets angry and asked him who forced him to marry her. She is also annoyed and insulted as he is flirting with his ex-girlfriends in front of her. When Sunaina asked him that why he is doing so and if he still loves his ex- girlfriend then why he wants to marry her. Abhay replied that if he had no issue with her boyfriend then why she is having issues with his ex-girlfriends. Again he said, he is not serious with these girls and so they are his ex but he is serious about her so he is going to marry her. Sunaina asked him again, *"I am not convinced so tell me five points why you want to marry me?"* Abhay replied, *"I want to marry you because you belong to a reputed family which matches our status, your engineering degree will be helpful in my business growth, our family know each other, you are broad minded and lastly you are pretty."* He was overly drunk that day and in unconscious state of mind he told her that he likes open relationship with her wife in which he can meet his girlfriends in front of her and if she wants to meet any guy, he will not obstruct her. He also told that he belongs to a high class society where this type of relationship is normal and she should mold herself according to this lifestyle. After saying all these he tried to abuse her physically which annoyed her and because of his misbehavior, she left the party immediately without telling anyone not even Ruhani. Sunaina is crying whole night and she has shared this incident to her mother and told her that she will not meet him again in her life. She told her mother that Abhay and Kabir are like two opposite poles. She also told her that Abhay has abused her and want open relationship in future. He is a self-centered person who has never bother about anyone's feelings, she said to her. She also told her that he had insulted her in front of his friends to take revenge with her as she told him about Kabir which hurts his fragile ego. She said, *"Unlike Kabir, he doesn't know how to behave with girls and to insult me, he was flirting with his ex-girlfriends in front of all and he is not respecting any women even his mother. And most important, he had invited us intentionally in his birthday party so that he could misbehave with me which is not acceptable."* Sunaina again felt like being cheated and a dumb whom anyone can make fool.

Love Note: True Love is an emotion and a feeling. Physical attraction and ego game is something else but not love for sure.

Love Test

Sunaina after experiencing so much worst in such a short life span, she wishes to move on from all this except Kabir. She likes company of Kabir and missed him all the time in his absence. She finds Kabir as a home where one get mental peace. She believes that Kabir will never hurt her but due to so many worst experiences she wants to test him before any commitment. In eight to nine months, she gets adapted with him. While Kabir had done his responsibility perfectly whether its pick up and drop service or bringing breakfast for her in weekends or giving dinner meal packets every day, coffee date every evening, movies and dinner in weekends, talking to her every single night until she slept. All these had left strong impression on her heart and which is obviously non resistible for any person. She enjoyed being with him because she doesn't have to pretend anything or she could be the real version of herself. And a year of happily passed like these. To test his patience, she let him wait all the time she met him but Kabir never loose his patience and temper on her. One day when they went to a restaurant, few guys are teasing Sunaina sitting in front of her. Sunaina thought that Kabir might get angry and fight with them but she got surprised that Kabir exchange his seat with her so that they can't tease her. Sunaina also tested him by flirting with him and giving him chance but Kabir never used any of her chances and never misbehaved. One day Sunaina tied a heart shaped balloon on his bike's back seat handle and told him to drive like this up to his home. He is not allowed to untie the balloon until reaching home and it shouldn't get burst while driving and show her that ballon in video call after reaching home. She told him that this balloon is her heart so if it burst on the way, then she will not meet him again. She asked him to do silly things like dancing on the road, singing inside the mall to check his commitment level.

Sunaina also tried to tell him about her past but Kabir never took any interest in her past life so he never asked her anything. Sunaina told him that she wants to talk to his parents and get confirmed that Kabir had informed them about her or not. Kabir did everything whatever she told him to do as he is also understanding that she is doing all this to build trust on him. One day Sunaina called Kabir to help her in finding a top in a branded showroom nearby her office. She told him that she had trialed this top fifteen days back and she liked it so much but she couldn't buy it because it's expensive and she didn't had money on that day but now she got her salary and she wants to buy that top. She challenged him to find out that same top if he really loves her. And after searching for one hour, luckily Kabir has found that top and proposed her again for marriage. But as usual she replied that her family will not accept him. Kabir asked her why her family will not accept, within a year he will be an engineer and also would start earning. She replied that he is one year younger than her. Currently she is working and he is a student. They belongs to different states, different cultures, rituals and beliefs. Her family wants a settled guy as her life-partner and finally some astrological things that her family believes a lot.

Kabir had listened all her excuses sincerely and then replied that he will do anything to convince her parents and marry her with their permission. He promised her that he will complete his degree in one go and will start job without going for higher studies. He told her that his parents don't believe astrological things in love marriage and they don't bother about our age difference. For them mental compatibility matters.

One day Sunaina's father got ill and her family members again started pressurizing her to get married so that her father could attend her marriage. Sunaina gets emotionally weak and decided to quit her job and shift to her native place. Now she have decided to tell her father about Kabir. And before telling her father, she also wants to do the last love test which is a loyalty test. So to test his loyalty she thought long distance relationship is the best idea.

So one day after office they went to beach where she told him about her father's condition and so she is going to quit her job and going back to her native place. If he wants to have another girlfriend then he is allowed to do so, she told him. Kabir smiled and replied *"Are you bored of me? So you are escaping from me"*. She replied, "*No I am not bored of you rather I am still in Chennai because of you but now situation is different and I have to be nearby my father.*" On this words, he kept silent for a while and then told her to go to her home and take care of her father. He told her that he loves her a lot and can't imagine his life without her. Sunaina asked him also to say five points why he wants to marry her. Kabir replied, *"I love you as you are and so I want to marry you. I loved everything related to you and care for you all the time."*

After hearing these, Sunaina hugged him and kissed him on cheeks. Kabir also gets emotional and kissed her on lips. After few seconds, Sunaina realized that she kissed him and felt awkward to stand there. Kabir made her relaxed by saying that sometimes this may happen in big cities and there is nothing to feel awkward. Nothing wrong happened between them, he said. But Sunaina remain silent and moved towards his bike and told him to drop her to the hostel. Sunaina kept silent all the way and Kabir keeps on talking to make her feel normal so that they could be friend like earlier.

Sunaina felt ashamed of her desperate behavior and felt awkward by thinking that what Kabir will think of her. After reaching hostel, she didn't talk to him even in phone. So next day morning Kabir has sent her a bunch of yellow rose's bouquet and a sorry note for his behavior last night. Sunaina smiled when she saw these flowers and called him to ask why he has sent her yellow roses, usually boyfriend send red roses to their girlfriends. Kabir replied her that first he wants his friend back then he will think about his girlfriend. Sunaina loved him more for his small gestures like this.

After that day, they get emotionally closer than before and Sunaina's decision gets firmed of telling her father about him. She realizes that if she wouldn't marry him then she have to regret in future. She knows that there are many social challenges but she have decided that at least she will try once so that she won't regret of failure without trying and it will be not fair to loose him without doing any effort.

Love Note: Love is a feeling but in real life people are different and have different intentions so testing someone is not a bad idea before stepping ahead in any relationship. All of us have some qualities and flaws so if you can adjust with someone's flaws then only you can maintain the relation happily forever. Everyone have different aspects from their life so before checking someone's qualities check his/her bad habits and if you have no issues with his/her that particular bad habit then only he/she is perfect for you.

Love to Marriage

Kabir has cleared his exams and for clearing his exams Sunaina and Kabir both have done equal efforts. Sunaina has given him targets and challenges that if he loves her truly than he have to clear all his back papers and current papers in one go because she don't have much years to get married as her father is also not well. So either he have to pass all his papers in current year or forget her. She told him that her parents were searching settled groom for her and if he couldn't start working then her parents will not accept him as groom. She wake up him every day at 5:30 a.m. so that he could study for his final exams and guide him in all possible ways. He had also tried his level best to clear 36 papers including back papers in one attempt and finally miracle happened, Kabir had passed all his papers with excellent grades. He called her immediately to tell her this good news. Sunaina's eye's filled with tears and her heart filled with proud for him. Now she is more confident of him that he could overcome other challenges too. She told him that her parents want a settled groom for her so he has to search job as soon as possible. Sunaina told her parents about Kabir's result and expecting that they will accept him but in reality this is not enough for them.

After few days, suddenly her father have to go to Chennai for medical checkup. He went there along with Sunaina's mother, sister and one of her maternal uncle. Sunaina told Kabir to take care of them in Chennai and may be these will turn into an opportunity to impress them. As she told, Kabir went to receive them at the airport and take them to their hotel and then doing every possible things to make them comfortable. Because of his infinity efforts, her parent's trip to Chennai and medical checkup smoothly done. While returning back, her uncle invited him to their hometown and offered him to stay at their home for a week. Three months later after finishing all his pending works, Kabir came to their home for a week. In those 6-7 days, he has impressed all her relatives and parents by his well-behaved manner and sincerity but Sunaina's father was concerned that if these boy came for their daughter than he is not settled yet and also younger than their daughter. Sunaina's mother likes him but couldn't accept him as son in law because he is one year younger than Sunaina which is not normal in their society. Her mother thinks how a guy younger than her daughter could manage all the responsibilities after marriage. But when Sunaina observed that he is very much comfortable with her family and vice versa, she feel secure about her selection and her decision gets firm that he is the right person for her and her family. After a week when he left her place for his hometown, Sunaina felt the pain of loosing him for the first time. She goes to see off him without realizing that she is falling in love with him so deeply that she couldn't see him going far away from her. She cried in railway station in public which is absolutely opposite to her behavior as she is always conscious about public dramas. She thinks many others came to her life and separated but she never felt fear of loosing anyone.

She cried earlier also but for betrayal, cheat, breaking of self-esteem but not for a loyal one and neither feel as she is feeling now.

Everyone in her family and relatives noticed that she is grown up now and ready for marriage. She gets numerous marriage proposals from her relatives and family friends. Those guys are well settled and ready for immediate marriage. Sunaina is worried for Kabir as he is not settled yet and Kabir is worried because he is not getting any job after completing his graduation.

Sunaina keeps on rejecting marriage proposals which her family and relatives brought to her. Some of these proposals are from her parent's friend circle and others are random unknown. To escape from these and being available 24 hours at home, she had started working in a company at minimum wages. She told her mother about her feelings for Kabir and also that she will wait till he settled in a job. Kabir had already convinced his mother and most of his family members for their marriage. Sunaina's family members are impressed by his behavior but still they can't think about their marriage as he is younger than her, not settled yet and childish in nature. Sunaina had a privileged life and so she is impractical and emotional in most of her decisions. She had never faced any financial crisis so her parents are worried if she will get married to a non- settled guy than how would she manage financial instability after marriage.

Meanwhile Sunaina pressurized Kabir that he brings his parents to her home for discussing their marriage and finalize the wedding date. She told him about her efforts in rejecting other marriage proposals by telling them non-reliable excuses. She is rejecting them by saying irrelevant excuses like rejecting a 5ft 10inch tall guy by saying that he is not tall enough, again rejecting another one by saying that he is not smart enough because he doesn't know how to take selfie. She rejects one by saying that he is not rich enough as he don't know how to show off his wealth and heights of rejection excuse is happened when she rejects an IITian by saying that he seems less educated as he don't look smart.

One day she pressurized him to the extent by telling him that she will marry someone else if he will not talk to her parents. Kabir can't handle her pressure and finally called her uncle and told him that he wants to marry Sunaina if they all agreed. Sunaina's uncle liked him from Chennai and he was the one who had invited him so he likes him but Sunaina's parent's permission is must. Sunaina's uncle told their conversation to Sunaina's parent and asked them to think about Kabir's marriage proposal. He asked Sunaina and her father about their opinion about Kabir. Sunaina's mother gets relief as her brother (Sunaina's uncle) agreed for Sunaina's marriage with Kabir and she doesn't have to convince anyone. She immediately replied that she is also agreed to these proposal. When all gets ready for their marriage then Sunaina's father also gets convinced for their marriage. Now all are almost convinced but no one is taking initial step. Sunaina again started pressurizing Kabir to talk to his parents and send them to her house. In India, this is a tough decision for any marriage that whose side will take initial step. Here both side parents expect that the other side will do the initial step and come first. After waiting for two months, Sunaina starts pressurizing him again and so Kabir pressurized his parents to initiate and go first. Finally his parents agreed and meet Sunaina's parents at her place and finalize their engagement and wedding date.

As Sunaina is earning more than him so she heard a lot of comments from her friends and colleagues that guys never tolerate if their wife getting higher pay than them. Mostly it end ups in daily fights. While Sunaina believes that Kabir is a hard worker and he will earn more than her someday as nothing is impossible for him. And her strong beliefs and determination manifest their luck as Kabir got promotion and his salary gets doubled just before their engagement day.

Sunaina's parents have faith in astrological match making so they called their family Guruji to match their *kundlis* whether they are astrologically compatible or not. Sunaina gets scared if that Guruji will say something negative about their marriage life. So she meet that Guruji one day before and told him that she loves Kabir and want to marry him. She has requested Guruji that he will only tell the positive things about their marriage life in front of her parents. Next day when Guruji came to their home and match their kundlis, it actually matched 36 out of 36 *gunas* so Guruji has nothing to lie about and he finalize the dates of engagement after two months and wedding date after six months of courtship period.

After such a long struggle and confusions in their life finally they get married with mix rituals of two different cultures and states. Both of them are happy and thankful that their dream of living together comes true. Kabir got promotion again after one year of his marriage and bought a car for her so that she could live her life like before. Both of them do job in their own field and work hard to achieve their goal together. On their second anniversary, they bought an apartment together and achieved milestones one after another. In these two years of marriage life, they have disagreements, argues but love overpowered all. They had struggled in jobs but achieved more. They compete each other in earning but support each other more. Sunaina fixed some rules for their home to avoid disputes like whatever they both may earn that will be the total income of their home and not individual and someday if they fought, it will not linger till next day.

After two years of their marriage, Sunaina's parents get to know about that past Guruji incident. So they call another astrologer to see their *kundlis*. Its surprises them all that after all such manipulating things done by Sunaina to marry him, unknowingly their *kundlis* are already compatible and doesn't need any manipulation and this is what we called couple made in heaven.

Actually we can't arrange or select our perfect match but it happens by its own and no one in these world can steal anyone's fortune. Whatever is written in destiny, one would get it at the right time. All who are in love, should keep patience and faith on their luck. You don't have to run after anyone but whoever is in your luck will appear automatically in your life at the decided period of your life. All the heartbreaks, cheats, pain, struggle in life are temporary as well as essential as it teaches us life lessons to make us stronger, braver and ready for life. The couple in this story are living and fulfilling their dreams together and these story is based on truth.

Love Note: True Love is above all and you will reach your destination anyhow. No one can stop you to get your part of luck. What is decided in your destiny will comes to you at right time, no need to worry unnecessary for that. Love has the power to prove wrong all the stereotype thinking. So have faith and stay happy. Good Luck !